THE VIGIL OF QUEBEC

FERNAND DUMONT

The Vigil of Quebec

TRANSLATED BY SHEILA FISCHMAN
AND RICHARD HOWARD

UNIVERSITY OF TORONTO PRESS

Originally published in 1971 as *La Vigile du Québec*
Copyright © 1971 Éditions Hurtubise, HMH Ltée
English translation (including new introduction,
'A letter to my English-speaking friends')
© University of Toronto Press 1974
Toronto and Buffalo
Printed in Canada
ISBN 0-8020-1976-5 (casebound)
ISBN 0-8020-6184-2 (paperbound)
LC 72-97423

This translation is published with the assistance
of a grant from the Canada Council.

Contents

F. DUMONT

A letter to my English-speaking friends

This book is not a portrait of Quebec. Nor does it even offer an explanation for the change in all areas that has characterized what is generally known as the 'Quiet Revolution.' I am concerned less with isolating the forces at work than with looking for the attitudes I ought to adopt as I confront the destiny of that fragile community which is my own.

Different approaches, more objective or more neutral, are certainly legitimate. In my practice of philosophy or sociology I frequently have occasion to employ them. However, the questions I was asking in these essays suggested another course. Is there any meaning in this history, this vigil of a paradoxical people? Is it worth keeping up? Questions of this kind are bound to involve the personal judgments of the questioner.

And it may be that there is no other way to communicate the perplexity of my countrymen to those outside the collectivity concerned – to you, in this case. This is naturally part of my thoughts as I read through the translation of my book intended for English-speaking readers by the University of Toronto Press. The change in audience means that my reflections are cut off from the ties and extensions that bind a work of this kind to its original soil. Speaking to my own people I had to assume many things, complicities and oppositions that were mysterious or familiar and that may be of the essence: for a country is first and foremost, to those drawing sustenance from it, a blend of signs that are present even at the centre of the most serious conflicts. Yet, all things considered, perhaps the worst possible way of winning our neighbours' comprehension would be to concoct explanations for their consumption only, omitting everything that would not be immediately intelligible on the basis of their own assumptions? Authentic dialogue implies for each the arduous task of getting right down to an understanding of the life-experience that has formed the motives of the other.

I fear neither of us, on one side or the other, has ever had the patience and courage to make this effort of feeling for the roots. I must stress this fact at the outset.

Painful though the admission may be, it must be said that our two peoples are relatively indifferent to one another. We have frequently come into collision or paused to exchange good wishes, but never have we felt for one another that deep fascination, whether of attraction or hatred, which characterized the relations between certain neighbouring nations elsewhere. Our confederation has often been described as a *mariage de raison*. The epithet is more unfortunate than our wise politicians perceive it to be. Such a 'marriage' can only join partners who are so remote that they can reach one another merely on the surface of existence, where there is nothing but episodic coincidence or conflict of interest.

This sort of tolerance does not make a country. We have managed to fool ourselves on this point for a long time, so completely were we living each on our own, looking to Mother France or Mother England, united superficially in fear of the American giant, brought together in the mixing of our business or political elites. But – and you sense this as well as we do – times have changed. Those outside alibis, the American menace and memory of the motherlands, are no longer very helpful to us. Whether our coexistence is to retain the shape of today's Canada or assume another, we face the inescapable job of building a community from within. I am convinced that the clearest minds, on your side as well as on ours, will agree readily on that.

But how are we to go about it, and with what materials? Bilingualism and multiculturalism? It is convenient for me to be able to ask for an official form or an airline ticket in French from time to time, but this deference to a basic right does not affect my sense of belonging to that community of ideals, ways of living, and feelings that makes a civilization and gives richness and range to its language. Bilingualism only connects us at the conventional surface of our respective languages. Even the widespread use of translation is an additional indication of what is keeping us apart in terms of a somewhat more genuine exchange between our two collectivities. It sanctifies the separation much more than doing away with it.

What can we offer one another that is more deeply part of our respective civilizations? This is the question we run up against in the end. And here are exposed, I believe, the contradictions and defeats of those currently responsible for Canadian policy. They alternate between two scenarios.

First, trying to unravel the traditional dilemma of our co-existence, they frequently discard the cultural fact, the tangled network of our individual ties, in the name of a purely rational and functional concept of political purpose: equalization of resources between the provinces, the rights of man, economic growth, etc. Yet in proposing solutions for these problems they are obliged to appeal to motives not found in the logical mind – a community ideal that can make the rich provinces willing to share with the poor ones, cause English-speakers to turn bilingual, induce various groups to accept the same concept of development for directing growth, and soon. In short, they use the cultural fact while claiming to deny its influence.

Second, they ask us all to put away our old quarrels and concentrate firmly on building the Canada of the future. Yet to bring us all together they cannot avoid evoking something of a common past: celebrating the centenary of Confederation or the anniversary of the provinces' entry into the great Canadian whole; placing Sir John A. Macdonald or Sir Wilfrid Laurier on our banknotes; parading Her Majesty and the emblems of empire throughout our lands, etc. In fact, they have taken on an impossible task – to sort out for us the good feelings from the bad, the good from the bad memories. A political decision cannot, in these matters, create a community that does not exist. Strategy cannot take the place of dialogue.

The game is not even new. We rerun, in fresh historical situations, the script that relegated us to the very estrangement and double solitude we want to escape. Even at the moment when the Canadian state emerged, was there any resemblance between the English-speaking Fathers' images of the country they were founding and those of the French-speaking Fathers? What similarity existed between the interpretations of Laurier's role accepted by our respective ancestors? Did we have similar views of Bourassa's 'Canadian nationalism'? Our attitudes to conscription in the world wars were even more revealing. We opposed one another, not only by a massive 'yes' or 'no,' but in obedience to fundamental approaches which meant the issue itself was stated in radically different terms for you and for us.

Nor are Mr Trudeau and the French-speaking members of his team the same for you as they are for us. This fact has nothing to do with the use of a duplicity I do not dream of ascribing to them, but arises rather from the varying refraction of their image and role in two different social milieux. On our side, we follow or oppose them primarily as participants in our family quarrels: when you assess them your different criteria do not overlap ours at all. I offer this in explanation of what happened in the 1972 federal election. The very different results in Quebec and a great part of the English-speaking country were not related, as some have said, to massive opposition against us. You voted for or against a Trudeau who is not the same as ours, just as our parents expressed their opinions on a war that was not the same to one side as it was to the other.

It is a game of symbols, and you will have no difficulty in recognizing its characteristic patterns and dilemmas in any of our so-called 'national' organizations and most of our encounters. More often than not, we attempt, by constitutions, regulations, compromises, and appeals for unity, to fit our two parts together in a superficial and shallow manner unrooted in actual conditions. For if the story of our political dialogue is one of failure, it is so primarily because the other dialogue, that of our two societies, our two cultures, has long been in a deadlock we hardly ever dare frankly consider.

Actually our ignorance of one another goes further back than our political divergences.

In the days after the Conquest the small French population spontaneously remained the same. Already distinct from the French of the mother country in social ties and ways of living, it was able to switch allegiances in the concert of empires; its coherence came chiefly from other factors. It was a coherence in day-to-day life untouched by the all-encompassing ideologies by which a society embraces a general image of its life and its peculiar qualities. Even when these ideologies began to form, particularly with the advent of the Assembly and the newspaper *Le*

Canadien, the uniqueness of this tiny people, like its survival, was not in doubt. Small though it was, moreover, that population made up an overwhelming majority in relation to the handful of civil servants, merchants, and camp-followers left behind by conquest and occupation. The distinction was preserved between the local agents of an extortionate oligarchy and the great democratic liberties inspired by England and the imperial authorities. Although the memory of France had naturally remained fresh and stirring, there was yet no regret for what was freely admitted to have been the authoritarian and arbitrary government of the *ancien régime*. It was with the increase of British immigration that we began to despair for the survival of our people, a despair that was to be reinforced by the Durham Report and the Act of Union.

From that time on, one was not dealing simply with a people colonized and later transferred to a new allegiance. One society faced another in the same land. One was primarily a peasant society, officered by an elite from a traditional milieu who remained faithful to its patterns of thought and action: the other presented a different structure and pursued a different ideal. Here is the origin of the lasting images of one another evolved in our societies, images which, with alterations in vocabulary and form, have continued in use up to our own time. In our view, your emphasis went chiefly to business and progress; you saw us as stick-in-the-muds, prisoners of our ignorance and archaic customs. Each built up his self-awareness in opposition to the image of himself transmitted by the other, with the result that our proximity made us more foreign to one another than some nations separated by geographical distance. Your ideal of progress was nourished by the contempt you felt for the negative example for which we provided the symbol. Our own uneasy uniqueness at last found its repose in traditionalism: what you saw as inferiority we made into a virtue. Mutual contempt acted as a guarantee for us both. And when we wanted to get together in spite of everything, we would simply invert the terms in the algebra of our mutual disdain: for you, our bemired traditionalism became an obliging folkloric vestige that helped give Canada its inextinguishable uniqueness vis-à-vis the United States, while your grasp on our economy served us as a concrete example when we wanted to 'adapt' ourselves to modern civilization.

Though it is still noticeable in so many encounters when we both play at dialogue, this age-old pattern has been in jeopardy since the

1960s. It has been the result not of new forms of dialogue but of rapid change in the society of Quebec. The Quiet Revolution has not only modified our social attitudes and structures; it has altered the bases of the awareness we have of ourselves. You would be taking a superficial view if you believed the new consciousness of Quebec involves an outburst of long-repressed hatred towards you: between the old images and the new ones forming, the usual meetings have become difficult. We can believe no longer, as the champions of *entente* so often tell us, that we only have to accept our differences and discover ourselves as we are. Since we decided to cease being what we were, it is comprehension of what we want to be that is now required of you.

What we want to be – we would first have to know what it is that we want to be ... And so I come to the basic theme of this book.

Since 1960, throughout that decade of Quebec's history that has been called the Quiet Revolution, you have been asking us, sometimes with irritation, sometimes with concern: 'What does Quebec want?' Always having locked us up in a convenient image, and now observing us getting under way after what you thought of as the stagnation of centuries, you would have preferred us to reveal some definite objectives. In reality the Revolution was not guided by well-defined objectives. Or rather, though it may have included some aims and plans that were consciously defined, this was only one of its aspects and certainly not the most important.

The largely artificial prosperity Quebec experienced after the last world war brought disorder to needs and aspirations that had long flowed in stabler channels. After 1960, needs and aspirations erupted into plain view with social movements of all kinds and sporadic demonstrations which naturally were difficult to define and describe. On another level, and in this case well before 1960, conventional manners and ideas had been challenged in art, literature, and ideology. No doubt these developments had a marginal air, masked as they were by the louder voices of religion and politics. During the last decade, these official philosophies were shaken. The crisis in religion was exposed for all to see, with a rapid decline in church attendance and tensions of all sorts within the Church itself. The meaning of politics was altered: not only were the grounds of Confederation itself threatened for the first time, but the very function of the State was subject to far-reaching examination. Political reforms were inspired by these changes in attitude and custom: in return, they accelerated in certain cases the changes in culture. The massive increase in school enrolment, for instance, has accentuated the gap between the generations.

Various, contradictory, and inadequately stated as all these impulses were, it is easy to understand our difficulty in reducing them to coherent diagnosis or political objectives. All this hardly gratifies your legitimate desire to understand us; it troubles us as well. Yet how could it be otherwise? A people in tutelage from their beginning, whose public face constantly hid more confused experiences and desires, has attempted self-expression by every means and all at the same time. We should not be astonished at the cacaphony that has emerged. A more coherent character can come only through this agony of utterance.

At least one observation may be made, fortunately, amid all this chaos: while appearing to abandon the patterns of their past, our people have been engaged for the past ten years in an extraordinary pilgrimage back to their origins. In popular song, in poetry, in historiography, and in many other areas, the Québécois are penetrating to the depths of their collective existence, and although they have never before demanded such an accounting of their traditional institutions, they have also never gone farther in expressing their need to regain the values inherent in the story of their own people. It is hard to disentangle even for inside observers. We alternate between self-criticism and the discovery of our special values. Our literature, our ideologies, as well as our daily conversation, waver endlessly between the blackest pessimism and the loftiest exaltation. A society in labour has a painful time giving birth to itself. Only politicians, accustomed to our old surface coherence or anxious to clothe us in an anonymous rationality, can imagine they might soon recompose us in lulling tranquility.

A people undergoing so complex a series of changes needs a collective endeavour suited to it, into which it can pour its emerging hopes, still delicate and ill-defined. In these terms, I believe, the great deficiency of the Quiet Revolution has gradually been exposed. As the years went by, political authorities demonstrated their inability to orient it towards objectives both broad and well defined. Beginning in the euphoria and dynamism of the Lesage government, the political experience of the party in power became consummated in the narrow ideals of managers, who, moreover, mask strategies and connivances worthy of the older politicos. This fall in the curve of political power could have been foreseen, in fact, right from the beginning of the Quiet Revolution.

For a century and more, in what looked like their long sleep, many Québécois had dreamed of 'adapting' to North American civilization. These fantasies grew more and more urgent after the last war. In 1960 a government took them over, and in various areas energetically tackled the jobs of clean-up and modernization. Yet can institutions be shaken up without confusion in attitudes and ways of living, or without disorientation for large sections of the population? Structural changes are easier to effect than changes in mentality. And so, as time went by, there came the nostalgia, the reserve, the slowdowns. Their effect was all the greater in that many of those initiating reform lacked what I like to call a 'pedagogy of change.' Their vision of the future consisted chiefly of catching up: their models – and tradition had accustomed us to this – were foreign to our society. In the field of education, for instance, learning had long been recognized as an important advantage, but as the ideal abruptly became fact, with the shocks and confusions that this inevitably entailed, there was anxiety among many of our compatriots; and, to relieve it, more was now needed than the example of others. What we needed was our own model for political and economic development. All we had was the formal ideal of modernization and the necessarily abstract example of success abroad.

This is the context in which we must view the events of October 1970, which gave rise to so much comment and were the pretext for publication of this work. It might seem that these events have exhausted their possibilities for the investigator. Of course, Mr Laporte has become topical again in recent months with the disclosure of his alleged connections with organized crime, and we were reminded that the circumstances of his death remain mysterious. But this is not the kind of actuality I want to talk about. The one that concerns me, and which retains its power, is not a matter of the factual unfolding of events. The FLQ represented no revolutionary force of any kind, though Mr Jean Marchand and company claimed at the time that it did. The Manifesto read on Radio Canada contained nothing that any citizen did not already know; nor did it offer any fresh objective. That happening could not be, in itself, the cause of a revolution. Like the storming of the Bastille or the Boston Tea Party, it was primarily symbolic. It was a backdrop, an atmosphere.

For a period of weeks the people of Quebec were drawn into a breathless self-examination, which Mr Laporte's death brought to a climax in a kind of collective trauma. The governments felt they had got out of their depth, less as a result of the problems raised by the kidnappings than by their impression that the indispensable social consensus was seriously weakened. The effect of the War Measures Act was not to untangle the affair, but rather to stifle rising public opinion, hitting at hundreds of politically minded people who had nothing to do with the FLQ or the kidnappings, and restoring order by an infusion of fear. The collective horror and remorse that followed Mr Laporte's death did the rest. The government's measures were no more the remedy for the crisis than the FLQ its cause. The problem is still with us, unscathed. One symptom, more striking than the others, was taken for the phenomenon. Even if there are no more spectacular crises, the transformation of Quebec's society is still feeling its way towards its outcome.

Our society can regain a degree of consensus, and confer shape on the new destiny to which it is bound after the disorder it has suffered, only through the involvement of its most fundamental values in new social and political structures. The nationalism and socialism that enter into the subject of this book have no other meaning.

When I talk about 'nationalism,' like many other Québécois I am not dreaming either of throwing up the barriers that formerly kept Quebec comfortable in her folklore, or of concealing under a national mask the problems relating to social classes and economic inequalities. I yield quite simply to one of the rare pieces of solid proof coming out of the Quiet Revolution. Abandoning decayed structures, our people have no choice but to call on their unique resources and pour them into an idea for development that is something else than the deceptive business of catching up with the others.

This same reason has led me to the ideal of political independence for Quebec. It is easy to make fun of Quebec independentists who want, as the phrase runs, 'to divorce Canada to marry him again afterwards.' No doubt the metaphor is comical, but the thought behind it is a bit scanty. What the new consciousness of the 1960s led us to challenge radically was not the idea of federation, which is in fact one of the great ideals of this century, but the caricature of it represented by the Canadian Confederation. Always, and more than ever during the past decade, we have had the conviction that we are a distinct people, and it is as a free people that we desire from now on to conclude our alliances, or, if you prefer the word, our federations. Moreover, the independentists are not the only ones shouting from the rooftops that the Canadian Confederation must be revised, that this state is too centralized, that politics are getting lost in constitutional battles and conferences that never come to anything. The necessary unity of the peoples of the world will never come through such imbroglio and it will never come through an abstract levelling of our differences. The state is not an administration superimposed on civilizations: to define those objectives that alone can allow us to overcome the complex problems of contemporary civilization, the state must call on the basic resources of the milieu where it must have its roots.

Our socialism desires the same type of substructure. The state, referring only to the liberal ideal, may certainly consider citizens as atoms moving in a society that is nothing more than a mechanical game. By contrast, attention to genuine inequalities, to the poor, the workers, and the underprivileged has always been the quality of socialism, however diverse may have been the ideologies it held. Moreover, it has perennially refused to treat the less fortunate as if any individual destinies had placed them in their position of inferiority: socialism has never misunderstood the weight of social structures and milieux or the existence of classes and powers. How could socialists, without contradicting themselves, disregard the variety of cultures? By definition socialist policy aims at closeness to the aspirations of the citizen, not only to make the State truer to the needs of men but to take from the latter that which can nourish political plans and endeavours.

I am quite aware that some of you frame these questions in similar terms. I was struck, among other such signs, by the emphasis placed by Mrs Kari Levitt, in her book on the power of multinational corporations in Canada, on the cultural aspects of this phenomenon: the supreme danger seems to her to lie in the manipulation of cultures, life-styles, and needs by these great foreign powers. She stresses that if we must resist them it is not simply out of a frivolous taste for economic autarchy, but because men should be free, beginning with their customs, their milieu,

and the solidarities that have made their history, to define their ways
and reasons for living. For the same motives, we believe that a true socialism cannot be implanted in Quebec without calling on the resources
of our own culture, and that it is there that it must first seek its strength
and its truth to the service of men.

I happen to believe that in following this path we may succeed in find-
ing the true channels for dialogue between our two peoples. Our questionings and our hopes as Québécois may often seem to you to indicate
a withdrawal into ourselves, an ethnocentricity that could cut us off
permanently from others, and from you in particular. But the long colo-
nialism we have gone through, our nostalgia and envy with regard to
France, the United States, and so many countries near and far – were
these not a pathetic warning to the world associated with a false awareness of ourselves? A people that will not grow up because it despises
itself makes a poor partner for anyone.

   Is this not basically your own problem also? And in this sense we are
more alike than we have cared to admit until now. You too are colo-
nials: lately second-class Britons, provincials in an empire where you
have never had much to say, now rehashed Americans of the second
rank. Do you not need to find yourself in your history and according
to your own plan?

   At any event, the hasty Confederation of 1867 brought together only
a few colonies. A hundred years later, is Canada in the process of becoming a frontier territory of the United States, its political unity but
the deceptive image of a hypothetical uniqueness? It is in regaining its
own essential quality that Quebec can best contribute to building something else in northern America than an outwork for the empire of the
United States. You cannot escape such a challenge. And is it not in following the search for ourselves, each of us on his own, that our two peoples can make a new alliance?

FERNAND DUMONT

THE VIGIL OF QUEBEC

Let us remember that sorrow alone can give birth to greatness and that the real way to restore our poor country is to show to her the depths that she is in. And let us remember above all that we cannot shed the claims of our nationality and the small notice that our country may take of our counsel does not absolve us from the duty of giving it.

ERNEST RENAN, *La Réforme intellectuelle et morale de la France*, 1871

It is my hope, in company with all my forebears who have hoped and with all those who hope today, my hope, beyond my time and all who have lost heart ... we shall have a country that displays her soul before the world.

LIONEL GROULX, *Directives*, 1937

Introduction

We are in the midst of a crisis whose outlines cannot yet be isolated, whose dénouement cannot be glimpsed. This will be news to no one: Quebec has been shaken up over the past ten years, far more so than most other societies. We have experienced rapid change, from at least seeming religious solidarity to rapid dechristianization, from ignorance to mass education, from Duplessis to independentism, from the challenges of *Cité libre* to the tutelage of Trudeau, and all this was enough to make any one feel that he had got lost in a time of general confusion. However, the autumn we lived through [in 1970] is traceable to a different anguish. Our destiny as a group seemed to elude those who, on one side or the other, had until then been free and able to explain it. With the implosion of the FLQ, the War Measures Act, and the death of Mr Laporte, it was not blood that 'flowed in the streets' as had been predicted, but fear, hatred, and foolishness.

During the past decade we have been asking a lot of questions about our collective weaknesses and the forces impeding us. Federalists have been particularly interested in the former, independentists in the latter. For both sides, there was a variety of interpretations that indicated an awareness of the subtleties involved. Despite our various forms of pessimism, our fate was within reach, open to considerations and commitments we could discuss. From our divergent and conflicting positions we had thought that we would be able to win the future we wanted through argument and patient anger.

4 THE VIGIL OF QUEBEC

And then, suddenly, fate came at us from the heavens. We saw choices forced on us that were founded on absurd rationales. It could have happened to any society; none has mastered the mysterious forces, needs, and ambitions that ferment within a society. Our own has said a lot about fate since 1960. We had apparently emerged from a long history (which used to be qualified by the dangerous word 'miracle') as one aroused from sleep. Fresh and ready like no other Western people, haunted by the accumulated dreams of a long night, we piled up plan upon plan in our hastily cleared house in that extraordinary morning of the 'Quiet Revolution.' Everything seemed possible. We set off in all directions, along paths others were exploring more slowly and carefully, marking the crossroads and dead ends on the map. It is true that we felt obliged to reach as soon as possible roads that were better drawn and that led to broader horizons. And soon we arrived at the point where Quebec found itself forced to choose among a variety of routes.

The choice was made for us. Some of our people wanted to force fate. We had two kidnappings and a murder. To some it seemed that this was the only way to re-establish political harmony, for that ideal was not sufficiently counter-balanced by slower, more discreet forces. They went so far as to believe that in order to free a people it was necessary to begin by terrorizing them. A different reasoning, equally rigid, opposed this one. In Quebec City and in Ottawa, sticks of dynamite stolen from various construction sites were added up until it was concluded that there was enough to blow up downtown Montreal. It would have made as much sense to add up all the hunting rifles sold during the last few years and to conclude that there existed a group of people better armed than the 22nd Regiment. One would have had to assume, obviously, that the purchasers had had no desire to kill partridge or moose but were devoting their time to exercises in anticipation of the final assault.

I will make only brief mention here of the conspiracy of which historians will one day give a final account – although I will speak of it in more detail later. For the moment, I would like to say only that the myths we thought we had lost when we emerged from our long sleep have returned – but this time we are awake.

What shall we do? Shall we argue until we are out of breath? Play the propaganda game that gets tougher until it all resembles police sum-

monses? Or plunge again into the waters of our special anguish? No.
There is one good fundamental thing that came out of this crisis: men
who yesterday were opposed on details that seemed to them questions
of principle found themselves spontaneously all solidly opposed to tests
of strength, no matter which side they came from. The only thing that
stood in opposition to the high and distant enactment of our destiny,
whether by terror or from political dens, was the defiance of those who
have always wanted simply to belong down here on earth.

When the 'crisis' of 1970 arose, I was in the middle of a course on the
history of ideas where I was supposed to be talking about Montaigne. I
was also spending the mornings working on a book about the relationships between 'theory and ideology' – both harmless subjects, of no immediate interest to either the FLQ or the police.
   During the 1950s a young man with any spirit of adventure would
never think of going in for politics. He would have big ideas about going
further than that. With the help of the quiet revolution a number of us
became engaged in scientific or philosophical research. We were naive
enough to think that the last barrier had been removed and that our
political evolution was taking place 'normally,' as you might say. We
were more attracted to problems of 'culture,' or to 'social' problems.
Politics mobilized us only on the side, and always with some hesitation.
Like many others, I spoke out against Bill 63[1] and shortly afterwards
took part in the election campaign – rather awkwardly, motivated by a
vague sense of duty. We had to move as swiftly as possible.
   Then in 1970 events swiftly brought us back again, more brutally
than ever, to face political reality. My students have helped to do this
too. Those of us in the CEGEPs and universities are accused by some of
indoctrinating the young. Those for whom I am responsible know that
during my lectures I have never been given to sermonizing, except at
times, I have to admit, about science, because rhetoric is one of the
temptations of our profession. But although I am a university professor,
I regard myself as an educator, much like a kindergarten teacher. Sometimes, after a discussion of a draft thesis, I find myself talking with my

1 Allowing parents to choose the language in which their children would be educated

students about marriage or the Christian faith or Quebec. We also meet at public demonstrations or more rarely in church – in the confrontations of this world or in our hope for another – side by side as free citizens of two worlds.

After the death of Mr Laporte students came to talk about the trauma that overwhelmed them, just as it overwhelmed my old parents and city-dwellers and country-dwellers alike. I try as best I can to lead them back to the hopes of our people. I do not want them to despair too quickly of Quebec, this insecure land of ours. Nor do I want the absurdity of our history to rush them towards either the mystique of the FLQ or premature withdrawal into a 'career' or into drugs.

To reassure us a little, I will recall the postures and ambitions of our past. The idea of publishing this book first came out of an examination of my own conscience. In the fifteen or so years that separate us from Duplessis and our youth, a number of men of my generation, on the threshold of vocations that were intended to be anything but political, tried to participate a little in the social movements working to build a new society. Ours was an intellectual participation, because that is where our competence lies. As far as I am concerned, my scattered comments over the years certainly do not make me worthy of the title 'theoretician of democracy' that some people have disdainfully bestowed on me. Even though I have written a considerable number of articles, it had not occurred to me to put some of them together, as I have now in the first three parts of this book, until some friends encouraged me to do so, thinking that they might provide some clues to what we have been saying and dreaming over the years.

In short, I thought, without going into it too deeply, that, faced with a threat that does not spring from within us, I could retrace my road to its starting point – a point at once very far away and very near. I would like others of my generation to do the same. It seems to me that, in the limited and panic-ridden present, each must tell his own story. It is rather like evenings in the old times when, in order to exorcise the storm raging outside, the old people would tell stories remembered from their past. This can work only temporarily, while we wait to get back our breath for future commitments that will be more difficult and complex.

In the fourth part of this book I have attempted to account for the 'crisis' of 1970 and what surrounded it. It is only a partial explanation, particularly because it is related to my own daily concern with cultural issues. Obviously there are other legitimate points of view. At the risk of disappointing the reader, I do not propose a series of measures that might guarantee the economic development of our country. I have examined the broader subjects of our present and future, the values that go beyond the area of technology to reunite with the goals that are after all our reasons for living together and living in Quebec. In these brief analyses, I have not concealed my own favoured options. On the other hand, I have not given in to invective, trying to remember that the highest ambition of our profession is understanding.

Understanding – how pretentious or, at best, how naive! In Quebec, reason is everywhere, on the surface at least. Against the flags and the signs, the authorities marshal reasoning to temper the dreams of a people always suspected of being unrealistic and inconsistent. In certain sections of the left I often encounter similar apologies for a rigid rationality: we lump together the old clergy, American imperialism, socialism, independence – all under the banner of ideological analysis and criticism. But always the residue is the same: feeling – although feelings are differently named and valued in each faction.

Intellectuals waver between two duties – creating theory and creating poetry. It is the custom now to separate into such categories all books written since the happy times of Plato, venerable forefather of all intellectuals, who could write freely in either mode, depending on the kind of proof his topic required. But in our present social and political psychologies reason and feeling cannot be delimited into separate territories; I strive therefore to stand on that hypothetical spot where our personal existence and the collective life that concerns us more closely can be reconciled and understood as one.

Thus I do not apologize for not having used here the last word in theoretical models or for not having produced a manifesto, since from my point of view understanding is an attempt to bring harmoniously together those matters which theories and manifestos properly ignore. This excuses too the fact that at times I repeat myself in this book. For the cohesion that each man, with his personal understandings and commitments, can give to his reason and feelings, cannot be developed with the single-line progression of theorems or have the perpetual newness of poems. We can only advance if we keep reviving and working over the themes of our greatest hopes.

PART ONE

A short account of our affections

The time of the elders

In the 1930s, at the time when Saint-Denys Garneau, Jean-Louis Gagnon, André Laurendeau, and others were beginning to do their writing, I was just a little boy, carefully protected from books by my working-class milieu. I was more concerned about stealing apples from the neighbouring farmers than participating in the intellectual or political confrontations of the period. As I develop, however, I feel myself increasingly involved in those past events. They have changed, but only in appearance. Today, like yesterday, we are circling the same difficulty or *empêchement* (the term is that of Jean Le Moyne): we are always prowling around an unfinished criticism and an unfinished problem that concerns my generation just as much as it did Saint-Denys Garneau and his contemporaries.

If I had to describe that period of the thirties as a whole, I would speak of it as the agonizing conclusion to a long story – the story of a certain traditional style of speaking that was imposed on us, as was a certain kind of silence, which I think can be defined by various signs.

Let us begin with the highest plane of verbal expression, literature. Saint-Denys Garneau belonged to a vast family, that of Ringuet, Savard, Grignon, and others. What did they have in common? They arraigned the traditional mythologies, thanks to the mythologies themselves, by taking up the old myths of this country and reworking and re-testing them in novels or poems. It was a strange trial where, behind the writers, the accused was the accuser and denials were also secret apologies. Ringuet and Grignon brought the bucolics back to the brutality hidden in peasant existence; on the other side, Félix-Antoine Savard's *Menaud: maître-draveur* (1937) took traditional mythology to its limit, the age-old dream finally discovering its truth, and its measure, in the character's madness. Whatever the route taken, our common heritage was not grossly discredited, though it was raised again by renewed interest in its more profound implications.

The same kind of development occurred with Saint-Denys Garneau and the group of *La Relève*. They were searching within the bounds of

Paper given at a seminar on Saint-Denys Garneau at the University of Montreal in November 1968 and published in *Études françaises* V, 4 (1969)

institutionalized religion; the diluted 'spirituality' that had hampered our lives was subjected to criticism and at the same time pursued. There are numerous examples of the use of traditional sources even in the denunciation that was made of that debased spirituality. For example, in 'Préliminaires à un manifeste pour la patrie' published by *La Relève* in 1936 we read: 'Patriotism assumes its true meaning and its true value only when it is subject to a Christian system ... to a Christian notion of humanism.'

Do we not find this continuity and this breaking with the past in every historical period? Are they not the very stuff of history? But here, during the thirties, this combination seemed to be building up to a crisis. It was not the sudden death of tradition that was being broadcast, but rather its interminable agony, an agony that continues still, after lending a tragic and lasting significance to the poems of Garneau, the novels of Elie and Charbonneau, and the essays of Le Moyne.

On the other hand there were also thinkers and writers who wanted to start off, as fast as they could go, towards what they called 'reality,' 'life.' They also called it 'politics.'

We must not hide this dichotomy in Saint-Denys Garneau's generation. But I wonder if a closer examination of the current bearing Jean-Louis Gagnon, for example, might not uncover a fluctuation rather like the one I believe I have picked out. Thus the political ideas of *La Nation* reveal not only a desire to break with the politics of the past but also acquiescence in the old dreams that were supposed to be shattered when they were brought into effect. It was probably Laurendeau who expressed this combination most perfectly in his writings and his personal history.

We should not try to minimize that part which amounted to an attempt at a total break: nonetheless, I doubt whether anyone stood by it completely and constantly. In that regard the late confrontations with the Duplessis machine offer their own statement. Men of my age took only a small part in them, but we were old enough to applaud from the depths of our *collèges*. Some of us experienced, in turn, the heady temptation to abandon the whole business. We too had been burdened with ideologies, morality, and false consciousness; we wanted to exist without ideology, living life to the full, amid the novelty and uncertainty of love, politics, and writing. But by rejecting this caricature of nationalism under Duplessis, we did not bring about our immediate liberation. We were turned back to the old heritage, to a more determined attempt to decipher it, although we still have trouble spelling the first words of it. We still feel, as our elders did, that the old vocabulary was counterfeit; victims of the same contradiction, we believe with them that the old silences – all those things our fathers did not say – should give nourishment to the new words we want to utter.

This remains, today as in the time of Saint-Denys Garneau, a middle-class complaint. Perhaps, though, I should qualify that, for when I recall my childhood lived far removed from books and the city, I seem to remember a drama similar to the one I have just evoked. I heard similar challenges to the old customs, to the old priests and politicians, but in a language different from that of the writers. Our fathers kicked and complained for centuries; they were not the docile sheep that have so often been described to us. But the crash of 1929 shocked us more conclusively. The proletarians who were Saint-Denys Garneau's contemporaries may not have caused a revolution, but they did bequeath to their children a new scepticism, a radically critical attitude, and a passionate anger that had something in common with the writers of the time. The centuries-old accumulation of bitterness among the working class burst like a ripe abscess. The words of an illiterate people began to penetrate the silence of generations.

This mixture of the old and the new had to be ambiguous. This ambiguity was exposed by our elders in the 1930s.

It would be easy to see in them what psychiatrists call defeatism. The generation of the thirties made our culture and our society look like a huge and historic shipwreck. They suddenly went back to their beginnings, and brought back a history already long. In this sense, the thirties have not yet ended. We know the themes of their complaint, the theses of their case: the accusation of politicians and political byplay; a willingness to substitute concrete analysis for idle chitchat; a denial of the myths of settlement, of agricultural alibis; the rejection of the trauma of conquest; tougher and more realistic versions of the old anguish of separation from Mother France and of the myth of our beginnings; and a painful rejection of a certain religion, the deepest expression of our self-dispossession.

All this criticism and analysis of our society's soul was bound to go on and on. Our contemporary literature is still battening on it. Have we come out of it all yet? When Pierre Trudeau, in the introduction to *La Grève de l'amiante* (*The Asbestos Strike*), amassed a terrible indictment of our traditional political and social thinking, the only conclusion he could find was the following: 'In politics, French Canadians have always thought with their feet.' For his part, Jean Le Moyne, in a well-known study of Saint-Denys Garneau, evoked 'the oldest, the most subtle, the richest of heresies: that of dualism.' These statements do not satisfy me: they take us too far back, either down towards our feet or towards the ancient history of the Church; too far from the mystery of our community.

So I come back to my starting point. Saint-Denys Garneau's generation became agonizingly aware that it was part of a people forever up against its own inexpressibility and incapable of giving it a name and knowing itself. We have traditionally made use of a language other than our own. I have been studying the ideologies of the nineteenth century in Quebec in a seminar composed of sociologists and historians. We were bewildered by the total lack of originality in the newspapers of the left as well as those of the right – there is nothing but finery borrowed in France or elsewhere, appropriated from a history that was not of our own sensibility. It is hardly necessary to recall that this was long the case with our novels and our poetry.

Here lies the meaning of the quest of Saint-Denys Garneau's generation, and the significance of his charge: 'They have trodden it down, without even seeming to do so ... / simply with their terrible and foreign mystery.'

We are this mystery. The generation of the thirties began the process of recovery because it at last dared aim at living awareness. This is what we owe to the generation of Saint-Denys Garneau, Laurendeau, Elie, Le Moyne, Gagnon, and so many others. Ours is not the joy stolen from Saint-Denys Garneau or the life Jean-Louis Gagnon tried to ensnare. We pursue the joy and the life still, in the promise of a fresh utterance that began with them. The clumsy devotion we give them may bear witness that their youth's quest was not without a future.

After the war: the search for a new awareness

When the war broke out in 1939 powerful forces of change were at work in our midst, but for a long time their activity was subterranean. We did not become really aware of them until the period from 1940 to 1960, and men in our society are still busy looking for the consequences of these changes.

We talk about urbanization and industrialization as a general indication of these mysterious forces. It is important always to stress the extraordinary suddenness of these phenomena in our midst and how weak were the means, psychological as well as economic, available to deal with them. Industry did not arise from home-grown maturation but from the meeting of foreign capital with our own natural resources. We had no economic power of our own, or very little: the major decisions were the joint task of foreign capitalists and indigenous politicians. We supplied the manpower. Our population was largely rural, docile, rather at a loss in a hastily constructed urban landscape.

The Depression came upon us as we were transforming our social structures. Rural emigration had been allayed and our countryside was retiring within its shaky defences. There was a considerable amount of urban unemployment. Farmers and labourers had no understanding of the cataclysm, but their peasant roots helped them ride out the storm. Memory takes me back to earliest childhood: in the close-knit clan formed by my parents' families everyone worked in a factory, but sporadically, and for very small salaries. Yet everyday solidarity, the old customs transplanted from the country to the city, the popular humour always tinged slightly with melancholy, helped make poverty bearable. We lived on the fringe of the greater society, which did not interest us enough to make us really try to understand it. From time to time a sudden burst of anger against the *Anglais* or the capitalists would shake the old servitude, but our enduring patience would return almost immediately. Rather paradoxically, it is their inexhaustible reserve of rural virtues that made it possible for our people to endure the consequences of industrialization.

Paper written in 1966 that appeared in Pierre de Grandpré, *Histoire de la littérature française du Québec*, volume 3 (Beauchemin 1969)

It is not too hard to detect a deep similarity between these general attitudes and the broader trends of thought expressed before the war. Before industrialization (and before the Depression as well) how many nostalgic diagnoses were offered up to us! We have been too hard, no doubt, on the nationalism of earlier days – our *Semaines sociales,* the *École sociale populaire,* and so many doctrines that now seem so dowdy and old-fashioned. They were all ideologies of the impoverished; for, in the new situations, the intellectuals were as unprepared as the ordinary people. They too had drawn on the old reservoirs of traditional attitudes and thinking. We said, and correctly so, that they were unrealistic. But we took part in nothing of importance. Where could we have served our apprenticeship in the major currents and complex processes of history?

The Second World War does not seem to have been a decisive break. For some people it seems to have been a repetition of the previous one: the same propaganda, the same 'conscription crises.' Our accumulated experience did not provide the needed ability for complete assimilation of such an extraordinary event. It enabled some of us, but not the majority, to acquire a certain international awareness. The war improved our standard of living, but our life-styles barely changed.

Coming back in 1947 to Saint-Henri, the working-class Montreal neighbourhood she had described at the outbreak of war in *Bonheur d'occasion (The Tin Flute),* Gabrielle Roy found her character Rose-Anna, whose thoughts were unchanged.

> *'The workers are earning a lot of money,' Rose-Anna heard people saying all around her, 'Soon they'll ruin industry, upset the whole economy.' 'Still, it's funny,' Rose-Anna thought, 'that it's always the workers who are to blame when prices go up or when the economy is overturned. Why not blame all those invisible people too, the ones it's so hard to picture behind the high walls of their mills and factories in Saint-Henri, far away from the walls of smoke and steam and the noise of the machines?' But Rose-Anna got lost in these considerations. She fell back on what affected her most closely: sixteen cents for a quart of milk; meat at prices she could barely afford; shoes that cost 50 per cent more than they had; even the price of bread had gone up ... 'How can the world go on like this?' Rose-Anna wonders as she walks past the church of St*

Thomas Aquinas: 'My God, how can the world go on like this? Is it going to change one of these days?'

My mother was saying the same thing in those days.

But this was the end of a world. We have to recall the time before the war to understand something about the last twenty-five years. Underneath the traditional defence mechanisms that crisis and war had stimulated among the ordinary people as well as the intellectuals, brand new experiences were taking root. We were to see them coming up, growing in the full light of day.

New generations have appeared, for whom urban life is the only life conceivable. Their acceptance or rejection of the conditions of life are not those of their parents. The old morality has been shaken, like the traditions that supported it. We have had to apply ourselves to painful reappraisals of our principles, religion, habits, the tiniest gestures of daily existence. Love, paternity, leisure – all became problems, all had to be reinvented. And we are not finished yet. Gilles Marcotte has said that our poetry is 'one of the first steps.' The same is true of our lives, even the most humble.

This new quest, with its tackings and hesitations, was manifested not only at the level of daily life but in the great social trends as well. One thinks at once of the union movement, which grew increasingly better organized between the wars. The growth of the Catholic Workers' Congress was less rapid than that of the other centrals: after the war, however, it exerted a special influence that was suited to our milieu. Shedding fairly quickly the old upholstery applied by our poor nationalist and clerical speculations of years gone by, it was deeply influenced nonetheless by some traditional characteristics: scorn for the big anonymous power-bases and concern for justice and equality. The CWC, today the *Confédération de syndicats nationaux* (CSN: Confederation of National Trade Unions – CNTU), was seen to be more aggressive than other social movements. For a number of workers, its importance was as a crucible for the transformation of old attitudes into new ones, with the latter drawing frequently on the vigour of the former. Various observers have already said that the significance of the Asbestos strike in 1949 cannot be overstated. On that occasion a whole class burst into the open with its presence, its strength, and will for change. Moreover,

because of repercussions in public opinion the strike made it possible
for many people across the entire province of Quebec to learn of problems that until then had been latent or disguised, and to make their own
decisions on the new alternatives. During these years the work of trade
unionism was still more basic: it represented the main opposition to the
archaic regime that ruled the State, and thus was a precursor for the renewal of our public institutions begun around 1960.

Similar transformations were at work in other social movements, in a
less spectacular way and without having reached the same maturity. A
new social elite has emerged from the *Action catholique*, the co-operative organizations, and certain agricultural movements. It is looking for
a co-ordinating ideology, hesitating as to which route to the future our
society should choose. But already a special style of commitment is per-
ceptible.

This background may help our understanding of the far-reaching ideological changes that have occurred since the forties. Three component
parts may be detached from all this, representing the fulfilment of previous trends and the uncertain quest for new themes.

The postwar years first witnessed the reduction of the nationalist tradition to abstract systems, as though its living sources had dried up. It
was the time of catechisms featuring the old clichés about our innate
Frenchness and Catholicism and the regenerating power of the soil. One
author, presenting a lengthy synthesis of this kind, wrote in 1946: 'This
book offers nothing new. It has one merit: it groups in a certain order
ideas that have been in our minds since the very beginning of our history – scattered, and without that direct relevance to the facts that
would give them value as directives – and that no one, to my knowledge,
has previously attempted to synthesize.' A summing up that was a liqui-
dator's inventory. What had previously been a tradition that was at least
partly alive was becoming a set of abstract conclusions. They could reveal neither reasons for living nor the face of our future.

The same could also be said of slogans circulated by the political party
in power at that moment. There is something horrible about this composition. Let me say immediately that we must allow no confusion between
men whose thinking was profoundly upright and certain political hangers-
on. But the remarks of Maurice Duplessis, who justified stagnation and
corruption with arguments claimed as originating from the traditions of

Quebec, made these traditions appear platitudes of no value at all in terms of a fair interpretation of our problems and our uncertainties.

It became normal from that time on to want to set aside all speculation at all coloured by bygone ideologies. As we had no thinking to replace them, there was at least a decade when some men knew the temptation of an ideological void. Setting aside traditional speculations, we went in search of an objective awareness. I would gladly cite this to explain the rise of the social sciences in our midst. For a long time we had fallen back on vague and abstract principles paired with an equally vague kind of sentimentality. We knew nothing, or very little, about our social and economic reality, about the phenomena of industrialization and urbanization that had made us foreign to the world and to ourselves. Suddenly, a positive search became our only recourse, a kind of zero point between past and future. And it was successfully incorporated in the social science faculty at Laval University.

When I first went there as a student in the fifties this was the discipline that commanded us. It must have been a terrible experience for our elders. For those of my age it was the most difficult and the healthiest period of our intellectual initiation. While the break with worn-out traditions was working in mysterious ways among the people, the *refus* was being drawn up in broad daylight, in a school. The attempt was necessary. But though the ideological void was an admirable gamble, it was impossible to hold on to. Science can only indicate some points of reference; it could not sort out those sources of energy needed, by societies as well as individuals, to initiate the search for a destiny.

We were committed, by inclination or necessity, to the paths of self-knowledge. We were not surprised that they were so diverse, and still are. Liberation of the inner life, the breathless search for new political structures, the confrontation between material and social technology – all that at once, often in the vaguest syncretism, still lies behind the ferment in our society. A society is being converted to its future. We will need much thought, and many novels and poems, to be able to meet the special challenge which was bequeathed us and which we are trying now to turn towards a vision of the world that is our own.

So here we are – seeking a new society.

Many French Canadians, regardless of their partisan loyalties, feel that they are witnessing some decisive changes in the world of politics. The

State of Quebec has taken on a new, youthful aspect. However, its future aims are still only partly defined. The most we can claim to have are fragmentary plans, and their foundations are shaky. However effervescent it may be, our political thinking has not found bases that are sufficiently broad and firm. The same thing might be said for our social movements. Some are attempting to renew their goals and their clientele, but the big decisions have not been taken. In the field of education, the revolution in progress is the necessary consequence of the crisis of conscience we have been experiencing since the forties. But to some it spells confusion, not only to those on the side of the state but to teachers at the secondary and university levels, and to the population as a whole.

In any event, our collective awareness has come up against the problem of assimilating the fundamental changes in our society. We see it in the ideological conflicts that assail us. Both the left and the right are uncertain of their traditions and their roots. The old nationalist themes turn up anew in counterpoint to such new themes as secularism and socialism. In fact, these old themes are renewing their deep-seated inspiration. We may reach the point where the past can regain its inspirational value. For the moment we have a variety of ideologies that are ill-equipped to reconcile contradictory purposes. No doubt we are thus playing our part in the anguish of all Western societies: living for a long time by great traditions, they are all now faced with the same challenge – the significance of economic progress. How do we rise above the wretched dreams of abundance? France, Germany, England, and the United States, taking very different routes and with a disquiet that seems less violent than our own, are experiencing torments familiar to ourselves. What vision of history are we to develop? What utopia can give our societies enthusiasm for the future? We are contacting a universal awareness, but by ways unforeseen.

It is this shared pain, our torments mingled with those of other peoples, that gives our generation its character and defines its task. It has also, since the war, given our literature its originality if not its quality. We have travelled a long way to awareness. We had been used to expressing our beliefs rather than our feelings. We used to write from the depths of our being, but from a distance, and we lived the same way. A first wave of novelists and a few playwrights (Roger Lemelin, Gabrielle Roy, Marcel Dubé, and others) tried to express the situation of the urban proletariat, lost between the old customs and the new world. Another group of no-velists (including Charbonneau, Élie, Giroux, Filiatrault, and Langevin) ventured into the area of personal drama and salvation, a quest that com-plements the preceding one.

And it was the time of poetry. The past fifteen years have seen an extraordinary flowering of poetry in Quebec. An uncertain society set off for the noblest of quests. Is the search individual or collective? It is impossible to settle it in these terms. When a society vacillates so be-tween past and future, when it is drawn by the ideological void and by objectivity, the individual is temporarily free of his roots, abandoned to a most personal anguish. For all this, poetry expresses the seeking and freedom of all: of Rose-Anna as well as Saint-Denys Garneau. This out-burst of language came suddenly for a people who have spoken so little and so timidly – and so badly, according to the linguists.

We must be extremely careful not to confuse this language obsession with foreign aesthetical preoccupations which, from Mallarmé to Barthes, express the troubled conscience and noble torments of contemporary lit-erature. Sometimes our writers borrow their justifications and their ex-planations from these themes, but they are mistaken in doing so. Our own themes are newer and more modest – more moving as well. We are trying to express and conjoin the silent nostalgia for the past and our utopian hopes for the future. That is why we proclaim our inner selves more successfully in our poetry than in our novels.

One Sunday my father took me on a familiar walk. We often used to make the pilgrimage to the working-class area where he spent twenty years of his life, where he experienced the first frenzy of love, and where I was born. That time we almost went and knocked on the door of the place where we used to live. But we turned quickly away – he reluctant no doubt to come face to face with a worker younger than himself, and I afraid to confront the living reproach of my childhood. But a little further on, as we looked back towards the large building where forty or so families still live, my father, who can only barely scratch out his name, challenged me: 'You know how to write; you have to put down all that ...' All that. It's pretty vague. But it is also important enough that we cannot yield to the temptation to hide be-hind a kind of scepticism that is not yet really ours.

After so much silence and so much stammering, we have at least one certain duty: to speak out.

PART TWO

Of a hesitant Quebec

A story of freedom

At first sight, we ought to make some kind of survey of the history of
French Canada, either to trace out a particular route taken by freedom
or to map or describe the obstacles in its way. In doing this in so little
space, one could only reveal one's prejudices and pin down with a handful of vague historical reminiscences the more or less arbitrary choices
we are now making. On the other hand, it is not at all clear that we have
to involve the past in any debate on freedom. I have the strong impression that, for many men of action among us, the appeal to history seems
a useless detour. They are all the more entitled to this reaction in that,
apart from national political action defined in terms of very formal democracy, our historiography conjures up scarcely any real capability to
inspire action among people of today.

I would like, then, to raise the anterior question. Why is our history
connected with our present activity, and does our history bring to us
the very basis of our struggle for liberty? Or, if you wish, what purpose
can our history serve for those members of our society in some sector
of our collective life who are trying to instil there certain values, spiritual or economic, intellectual or political, and whose work must feature
the promotion of liberty as one of the supreme values? To find an an-
swer we shall have to make a brief detour.

In broad sectors of French Canada we are seeing a ferment of liberty.
At the personal level, each person gets along with freedom: he makes a
coherent adventure of it or else a discontinuous chain of caprice. Yet
as soon as liberty is experienced inside a commitment, as soon as it is to
be installed in collectivities and institutions, we are looking for social
movements and organizations able to uphold their real aims of liberation.

In the present state of our collectivity, what are these social movements and organizations? They might be classified into four main groups:

This paper consists of a lecture given to the annual meeting of the Canadian Institute on Public Affairs in September 1959 under the title 'Does freedom have a
past and a future in French Canada?' to which has been added a brief extract
from a 1958 article. It will be noted that many of the hopes I expressed have been
realized since that time, but it seems to me that our historical awareness is still characterized by traits that I pointed out in 1959.

1   The trade union movement must occupy a place of privilege. It was certainly born of problems specific to our milieu, those we refer to habitually when we speak of industrialization. Here it takes on polyvalent functions: given our society's deficiencies, the union movement was led to give a voice to those who, though not workers, were unsatisfied with the conditions of social and political stagnation. That helped make the trade union movement a characteristic element of our collective life. Moreover, it has no *official* source in any of our traditions: it would not be difficult to show that nationalism – that of Henri Bourassa, for example – failed for a long time to recognize the unique quality of the trade union phenomenon. And the polyvalence we spoke of has limits: the union movement is too far from some social situations to give everyone a concrete rootedness. For some of us who are intellectuals, is not scoring the worker's struggles with rhetoric the substitute for a spiritual tradition that does not exist, or that we are not aware of in our own fields?

2   There are other associations, old or new, seeking coherent objectives. If we compare our milieu in this regard to others (American society, for instance), we realize that voluntary associations are relatively rare here. No doubt we are still tied to neighbourhood and family relations: we use a good many traditional patterns that make us think it inappropriate to invent new ones.

3   Opposition political parties or movements are looking for a very formal kind of democracy, in other words for a liberty whose content is poorly defined. In this connection many ask the question, 'Democracy – what for?' They then inevitably challenge the special significance of our milieu and its traditional values.

4   A few rare socialist currents are emerging hesitantly. One does not belittle them by noting that the great part of our population does not consider them their own and sees them as a kind of import. It seems incontrovertible that socialism has not been given the kind of colouring here that would let it put down roots. It seems impossible – even more impossible than in the union movement – to locate traditional sources for a Quebec kind of socialism. It would be superficial, in fact, to couple our old nineteenth-century political or religious liberalism to it.

This very brief inventory leads me to the formulation of some provisional suggestions. We have now and will have in the future more and more institutions that can serve as arenas for the exercise of freedom. Some of these institutions are intimately connected in their origins with our problems (unions, voluntary associations, etc.), while others have been borrowed from foreign versions of more universal problems: such is the case with socialism. This does not mean, of course, that socialist institutions do not relate to our own situation. What is lacking in the ideologies and organizations offering a collective exercise in liberty is that men from our milieu cannot achieve self-recognition in them. We lack a clear image of ourselves in the light of liberty; we have no definition of liberty that can be absorbed by the society we are forming. Here we are far removed from episodic struggles for civil rights, but we are on a plane that is just as comprehensible, where talk of day-to-day liberty calls us jointly and severally to produce a definition of the collectivity where the struggle takes place, as well as a definition of the values to bring forward in the circumstances.

This is what each of us must have when he sets out to grope for the points of contact between his desire for commitment and history as it is taking place. At the same time, we may be isolating the malaise of a society that is failing to escape its own stagnation, despite the action of militants from milieux of the working-class, agriculture, the co-operative movement, certain areas of political action, or the university: for that society does not find self-recognition in this activity, nor can it find a formula to express its own self-awareness.

Where are we to find this definition of ourselves? Or rather how are we to invent it in unison with the groups in which we are involved?

It will not be in any immediacy of action, in any event. For then we would produce only a series of airy-fairy ideologies, such as exist among us now anyhow. Men who live by the moment always elude our own present in the most distressingly abstract manner; if it were possible for us to find our identity in these 'immediate' labels, we would no doubt have done so in the years since they were first available.

In one sense the struggle for liberty means innovation, installing in the environment, near or distant, the values that are believed for themselves and liked also because they are new. The latter characteristic explains why so many of us talk about the 'fad for novelty.' The fad certainly exists, especially because here it finds no concrete pegs and so must become a kind of daydream. But we should remember too that novelty is inherent to values. Whether they be religious, political, or economic, values go beyond the immediate and the possible; he who has not heard the call to go beyond what is happening is not a bearer of values. Every struggle for values includes the struggle for liberty. In this sense, it is appropriate to refer to 'our master the future.'

But the future is not concrete. Utopia is made up from present and past. The 'rational being,' as our philosophy professors used appropriately to tell us, is made up of pieces borrowed from the real being. Counting only on visions of the future to justify the choices of today plunges us into the very abstractness we are attacking. We are too free of our anticipation for the future for it to appear as a collective image of society. A certain kind of Marxism very effectively illustrates the tyranny of obligatory images of the future. In our everyday commitments the 'rational beings' must remain personal productions – as in poetry.

This leaves us with only one way to find what we are looking for, and that is to imagine a certain drawing back from immediacy while at the same time remaining within the continuation of life-experience. Such an approach would give meaning to a collective sharing in the goals of the future, and yet not amount to propaganda. We are left with our past. The history of our ancestors is solid ground for deciding what we are. The past, like the future, enables us to test this feeling of the possible which is inherent in values. But in the past this test is a concrete one, going to the core of events, without much possibility of escape from the collectivity into pseudo-platonic universes. What we all feel deeply nostalgic about, both at times of doubt and at moments of exaltation, is that there is in our past a history of liberty. Without that invigorating self-knowledge which comes from it, our commitment can be only a delicate and uncertain personal aim or a search for opportunities. Such commitment is vacant and available like the liberty without content which waits every day for the morning paper before deciding what to be indignant about.

To grasp the profound importance of this history of liberty, it would be necessary to have felt something that does not occur very often in French Canada: how history leaps up at moments of crisis, when the immediate, the present, seizes one by the throat. One feels then the need for a certain distance, the need to retrieve a feeling of brotherhood with those who, in the past, foreshadowed our present fight. When

France collapsed in 1940, the spirit of 1789, 1830, and the Commune were revived with a new, young face. The collectivities were then feeling what each of us feels when, in hard times, we look avidly for the continuity of our past, the reasons why our choices and our confusion are not arbitrary. 'I write,' said Bernanos, from his exile in Brazil and from the chaos of a conquered France, 'I write for the child that I was.'

We have never lacked historians. Half of French-Canadian literature is made up of historical works or novels inspired by our past. Our poetry itself, that traditional channel of liberty, has long been based on historical themes. However, our history often seems like an initial obstacle in the way of liberty, like the wrappings of an embalmed mummy from which we have to be disentangled. Some people have the impression that they are free when they cast off this weight of the past. Why is there this contradiction – our need for history and our oppression by it?

The demands of a history of liberty run up against a long-standing French-Canadian historiography with a unilateral interpretative bias. The stress on the 1760 conquest, an essential point in the explanation of our history and one that exasperates some of our historians today, is not a recent thing. It has inspired all our Canadian history textbooks and goes back to our first great historian. François-Xavier Garneau, moreover, had taken it from a European French historian, Augustin Thierry. When we look for our past, we find ourselves faced with a tradition of our historians, rather than a national tradition. Despite everything, whether Garneau borrowed the central pattern of his historical vision or not, the idea of the conquest appears to have arisen in response to the situation of his period, to the crucial problems being raised by his contemporaries. The anecdote claiming that he decided to write our history in response to an insult from an English-language colleague may be only a legend, but it is an excellent mythic representation of the period. For the bourgeois elite of which Garneau was a marginal member, history meant the history of the *nation*, the only true French-Canadian community.

But this community has fallen apart since the nineteenth century. Our environment has become industrialized. The towns have taken on a new look. A working class has arisen for whom the traditional deification of the peasant made very little sense. Imagine one of today's militant workers who, having acquired some historical awareness, might look for the memory of those of old who had fought battles like his own. In libraries or in Canadian history textbooks for the period that saw the rise of our proletariat, he would find information on the defence of 'separate schools.'

So we grew incapable of asking new questions of the past. Our state of evolution remained essentially that of the men of 1840, despite the steady accumulation of footnotes. It bears repeating that our society, mores, and problems are changing, and the gap widens between our self-definition as passed on by exasperated historians or textbooks which never change and what we have become by the shaping of events and the new urban environment. I see in this the basic secret of our collective malaise whenever we think about liberty. To be able to respond to new situations, our version of liberty finds it necessary to repudiate the past because it has become a burden, a thing that can be analysed and discussed from the outside, as though it did not belong to the consciousness of each one of us. This quality has been accentuated in recent years by some of our historians. The traditional treatment of the conquest has become a real childhood trauma: hence the pessimistic nature of this point of view. Through a kind of psychological corollary that is almost unavoidable, this history-as-thing is deterministic. 'The historian is a seismography,' in the words of one of our finest scholars. And here we are trapped when we try to know ourselves.

Our historiography has not completely pulled out of this tradition, taken in the anthropologist's sense. There is the persistent image of a 'golden age,' in this case the French regime; the idea of a determining factor, unique and almost inevitable, the conquest of 1760; a unilateral definition of the collectivity as a community, a nation. A tradition that is archaic and collective in this sense cannot be truly alive in an urbanized and industrial society. If it survives, it is more or less as conformism, as an element foreign to what is lived. Historiography is not a substitute for tradition; it is its heir. It cannot be unilateral. In terms of the variety of situations, history must ask many questions, from many points of view. Max Weber stated it thus: 'The principles of the cultural sciences will continue to change in the future without limit, so long as a sclerosis of the life of the mind does not cause humanity, as in China, to lose the habit of asking new questions of a life that is inexhaustible.'

Our historiography should be psychoanalysed, so to speak. If we really want to read in our history about the progress of freedom, about spiritual traditions rather than a sociological tradition, the historian himself must find his own freedom again to face the past; and he must recognize, at the source of what he considers as the crucial events, the choices made by groups and historians before him.

The conquest is indeed a central event, but only if our history is taken solely as the development of a nation. Depending on whether we decide to read the past in terms of different kinds of solidarity – political, religious, workers' – other events will seem equally decisive.

In 1809, Denis-Benjamin Viger took a stand, in the first French-Canadian political pamphlet, against the tyranny of the French regime, and spoke the language of British liberty; some of our historians are no doubt ready to see him as a 'collaborator.'[1] In the text where Burke is so frequently evoked, I am tempted to see the discovery of a political community, the feeling of a civic responsibility for which I do not see the equivalent or even the possibility under the French regime. When I learn (not in the textbooks, obviously) that in 1775 a number of peasants were sensitive to the clamour for independence coming from the land to the south, I doubt very much whether those anonymous people were concerned merely with *la revanche des berceaux* and the preservation of our folklore. The 1837 adventure, the working out by French Canadians of the idea of Canadian independence, the already subtle thinking of the first militant workers from the international unions at the end of the last century – all that tends to make me think that our country has not been barren for liberty and that all the groups now struggling for certain values can find ancestors in our past. From a related viewpoint, it seems to me that one of the crucial tasks for our contemporary historiography would be to explore our recent past, say from 1875 to the present, when our milieu really stopped being 'traditional' and when a working class was born that, simply by existing, constitutes the greatest challenge to the national community. I do not make this statement to fill some kind of intellectual void in that universe of works

1 *Considérations sur les effets qu'ont produit en Canada, la conservation des établissements du pays, etc.* (Montreal, chez James Brown 1809), 38-9

about which we intellectuals think above all, alienated as we are somewhat by our trade and the bibliographies that it implies, but to fill a
spiritual void, the distance between what we have been and what we are.

I do not reject the interpretation of our history in terms of a national
past; I am willing to accept this along with other readings. A history of
Canada conceived in a polyvalent fashion would not make our past appear as the nightmare of an interminable dying; it would present various
faces of liberty. Those who, in the present, do not work on a plan of action that is strictly patriotic would then no longer be rootless in their
compatriots' eyes and their own.

Some may say that I ascribe too much importance to books about the
past. However, only the historian can psychoanalyse our unhappy consciousness and found our choices on integrity. The nation must become
the nation of all. For this to be true, for the worker as well as the intellectual to find self-recognition in a common destiny and a common
choice, it is no longer the *Anglais* but our class system that we must
attack. Here as elsewhere, nationalism has concealed the problems of
social inequality too long for us not to find, in this struggle for a deeper
sense of community, worthy tasks for man and the countenance of a native land that has at last become contemporary with ourselves.

Is there a future for the French Canadian?

For the moment, there is still a French Canadian. He is difficult to iso-
late and define – slightly more so, no doubt, than the American or the
Frenchman. But it is enough to travel in the Beauce or Charlevoix and
even in certain sections of our big cities to recognize this singular being,
and to feel one's own heart leap in that unmistakable way. Is there point
in this curious variety of human fauna continuing to exist? That is the
real question, the most trivial and the stupidest; but I am surprised not
to hear it more often in those debates that exhaust our emotional and
intellectual energies. The questions leading up to it are always a trifle
simplistic, but I may be allowed just the same to pause at one of them.

Article published in the special issue of *Le Devoir* commemorating the Centennial
of Canadian Confederation (30 June 1967) and reprinted in the journal *Esprit*
(July–August 1969)

One thing seems certain to me: the nationalist language and aims that have guided our thinking on these problems are largely out of date. A normal man could not recognize himself in the cultural, religious, economic, and political syntheses that only yesterday covered over all the deficiencies and dreams of the French Canadian. Between the federal minister, Jean Marchand, and some village politician who still sounds off the old nationalistic slogans, clearly the former is right from the outset. When Mr Marchand emphasizes that we are in the era of technology which, basically, recognizes no frontier, he gives me a useful reminder of the obvious.

But he brakes the development of his reasoning too rapidly. In this universal perspective I do not see what makes him stop at the Canadian border. Why should our children not simply be American? It is a serious question, and we have asked it here in every generation for over a century. As far as I am concerned, I do not feel any absolute opposition to the United States: their industrial power astonishes me, some of their universities inspire the greatest admiration in me, their literature interests me infinitely more than what comes from here or from Toronto. Of course, the American policy in Vietnam disgusts me, but Canada's policy does not seem to me to contain anything very original either. Frankly, to pass from the universality of a technological society's demands to the need to build a Canada in opposition to the United States seems a flagrant contradiction to me, and the ultimate in regionalist timidity. I do not see why we should not be content simply to shift the barriers, nor do I see anything that places Canada, as such, at serious variance with the United States or any need for the creation of a new nationalism. And so here we are, back at the question of a French Canada that no longer exists and a Canada that has not yet come into being. This is very disturbing for those who, like me, are at the mid-point of their lives.

I feel obliged to come back to the primary question of French Canada. People have made a lot of fuss about industrialization and urbanization in Quebec. We have heard how these changes have challenged the traditional modes of living and thinking, as do the ideologies in which we found the argument for our collective existence. The educational revolution now in progress will, perhaps, be equally important; in any case, it further extends, and in the same direction, a radical transformation of our milieu. If we have survived as a people, it is above all because of the isolation in which the mass of the people have been kept. In the days after the conquest, the seigniorial system separated us from our Anglo-Saxon neighbour. Afterwards, our country-dwellers lived on the fringe of the North American world. It was also the period when Quebec City considered itself 'the Athens of North America': this enraged Olivar Asselin, but reassured the others. Furthermore our collective ignorance preserved us. Even when we emigrated to the towns, our proletarian contingents were cooped up in neighbourhoods and in occupations where a more or less bastard but still distinctive language and mores were kept up. We should not speak too harshly of *joual*: it has been and is the most faithful companion and the most unbeatable evidence of our survival.

If the revolution in education succeeds, all that will quickly be disposed of. People will be better educated and there will be more technicians. But will they find normal working conditions in Quebec? And what is more important, will they perceive a rationale in survival of the French-Canadian type? I would bet the American empire would have a stronger attraction. And any improvement in the quality of our language would not be enough to slow down the movement. Language goes back to something else besides itself; it is the echo of a collectivity that is worthy of expression, that feels in it an irresistible urge and an irreplaceable joy.

Something of the same sort might be foreseen for intellectuals; those who, by definition, examine values. Until recently our elites found their food for thought in our difficulties themselves, as well as an easy way to justify not becoming attached to the more universal anguish and problems of the period. We made a vocation of doing our thinking strictly among ourselves. Some of us are already trying to work from other perspectives: those of science, of philosophy, of the world that is being created. Some of us have dreamed of going off to work more peacefully somewhere else, of not getting caught every morning in the local morass opened to us by the front page of the paper, of not floundering around ever again in the philosophy of such-and-such a provincial *député* or the political science of some eminent representative of federalism.

Not so very long ago, very few of us had the choice. However, we know that in the fields of big business and of scientific research many have emigrated in body or mind. From now on the possibility will be open to more and more French Canadians. Some will rejoice: 'each must count for one,' they tell us in those speeches where they can still stir up the old nationalism. But is this not a dangerous delusion? No nation is viable unless the group itself gives the individual the idea of basically belonging. France's future would be seriously jeopardized in our view if each Frenchman, at a certain point in his life, had to make a conscious choice in her favour. It will soon be that way here for all those who have picked up, along with their education, the ability to uproot themselves.

What has been truly decisive in the Quiet Revolution, in fact, was referable to culture: there was educational reform but there were also assorted dreams, the desire for new attitudes. The very formal ideologies where we had found our identity rapidly faded. Catholicism, for example, ceased to be the framework of our nationality. Many believers, of whom I am one, were delighted; we believe that pluralism is a happy conquest. But where are we now to find that certain unanimity without which no nation can exist? We have reached a point where we must find another collective project. Is it possible? That is the whole question, and constitutional arguments are meaningful only in relation to it. Time is pressing. We should already have some concrete achievements. The revolution in the schools seems to have been achieved. But where are our definitive choices in the areas of the economy, planning, development, scientific research? We are too quickly reduced to confused questionings that are translated immediately into narrowly political ideological conflicts.

Finally, at the bottom of it all there is a problem of conscience that has not been elucidated. I would like to say quite simply how I see the problem.

At the end of an article on the destiny of our whole civilization, Paul Ricoeur wrote: 'We must be progressive in politics and archaic in poetry.' I will comment in my fashion on these opposing and complementary notions. In theory, there could be no true politics from now on unless focused along the development tracks of contemporary industrial societies: everywhere the boldest planning and development procedures are to be put to work and national barriers are illusory except for reasons purely and simply out of the dictates of strategy and competition. But technology and planning by themselves could not identify collective ideals or reasons for living. Raising the standard of living is not even a primary criterion, either for individuals or for the collectivity. The wish to restrict oneself to supplying everyone with a certain security and an appropriate income is a direct continuation of the old liberalism. We assume that the individual has the capacity to select his own values, but this faculty does not exist if it cannot find support in a certain consensus with other people. This consensus is archaic in two ways: it appeals to forms of interdependence that have slowly been created by history; it has its roots in the deepest layers of the conscience where essential values and symbols are at work. Archaism and progressivism: that is the point of contact of poetry and technology, of love and the family budget, of values and planning. And equally, of national feelings and politics. Loyalty to the nation falls into the realm of the archaic, but as only one element of it, and probably not the most important. The loyalty issue is nonetheless one of the most easily accessible ways in which the community of values can define itself as the opposite of the organizations.

In this context, I for one believe in the virtue of small nations, where common values have the opportunity to sink deep roots. The desire to create a Canadian nation means attempting to put together an archaism, which is clearly absurd. There remains Canadian politics. I have trouble seeing what it adds to our destitution faced with the American mastodon. Nor can I see how this would create a bigger window on to the international scene for Quebec.

If I tend to lean towards the separatist solution, it is paradoxically in reaction to any kind of narrow nationalism, whether it comes from Quebec City or Ottawa. Quebec should avoid any useless detours and assert as quickly as possible its presence in the world. The flowering of our own still timid cultural values requires lots of air. The fertility of our own archaism is not found in opposition to English Canada or even to the Americans: it goes by way of Paris, Brussels, Algiers, Rabat, Tunis, through a geographical network where I do not see a place for Ottawa. If the Minister for External Affairs sees in this the incontrovertible dissolution of our federal ties, as he declared recently, I am sorry for him. But I can only ask myself, once again, what cultural ties bind us to Winnipeg or Toronto in so direct a manner that we should have to come to an agreement in order to define what our cultural growth has in common with that of France and Tunisia. After all, Canada is only one hundred years old, and I would like to emphasize this for any federalist

thinker who leaps easily from the nineteenth century to the twenty-first.
If we should maintain some tenuous link with Ottawa, and I have no im-
movable conviction one way or another in that regard, our only criterion
for doing so should be the incontestable progressivism of federal policies.
I have already stated that I do not see any tangible sign of this. I even
wonder whether Quebec's economic ties are not more universal than
those put together so incongruously by the federal government.

To return to essentials: can the French Canadians free their old loyalties from the old nationalism and with them give support to a collective
project that could make its small contribution to the enlightenment of
humanity? Only then would we have reasons for perpetuating the French-
Canadian species. For the moment, and I am not ashamed to admit this,
I am reduced like everyone else to the most elementary feelings on the
subject. When I observe the impotence and inconsistency of our political authorities, or get swamped in the morass of our domestic quarrels,
or see the time for decisive options in some area or another passing by,
I confess that I am pessimistic. Like many others of my generation I
have made my choice, because the age is coming when one can no longer
turn back and when one clings obstinately to jealous loyalties. I will continue to live, to love, to dream, to write in French Canada. I am not too
sure why. Perhaps it is in order not to betray some mysterious ideal
which comes from my illiterate ancestors and which, even if it were
never to take on a clear form, leads back to the most desperate definition of honour.

Canada and the United States: an ominous proximity

Three-fifths of Canada's production is at present under foreign control.
This is unique among all the industrialized nations. The United States
plays an enormous role in this economic dependence. In 1964 Canada's
total debt to other nations was $32.8 billion, if we include short-term
foreign investments and certain other liabilities. By 1967 this debt had
reached $36 billion, of which $30 billion was in the form of long-term
investments.

Article commissioned for *Le Monde diplomatique* (September 1967)

American investment in Canada is not, of course, a new phenomenon. It was already considerable at the beginning of the century, but so were British interests at that time. During the thirties America's share was approximately $5 billion. With the Second World War Canada reached a new and crucial stage in its industrialization and in its subjection to the United States. Its trade deficit became dangerously accentuated. In a courageous speech that created quite a stir, Mr Walter Gordon voiced his alarm: 'From 1958 to 1962 we had unused resources and a high rate of unemployment here. However, we continued to contract foreign debts and to sell Canadian companies in order to pay for our imports. This made no sense. In fact, we were importing unemployment.' And we are continuing to do so.

Moreover, a large portion of Canadian savings are invested in the United States: approximately three-quarters, we are told. Even Quebec, an industrialized province whose revenue is considerably lower than Ontario's, exports a great deal of capital. Stock-market investments and the draining of our savings by American insurance companies are obviously factors here.

An article in the December 1963 issue of *Fortune* magazine recognized quite casually that Canada is 'a country that American companies consider as an extension of their domestic market.' The same statement could be broadly applied in the area of culture. Canada is experiencing a serious lack of highly qualified researchers and technicians. But for some time we have been sending a good number to the United States. No doubt we must invoke the deficiencies of Canada's science policy, and those of the provinces. But, with very rare exceptions, the large American companies with branches in Canada have been very careful to establish their own large research centres. 'An extension of American territory,' perhaps, but a marginal zone – the first to be affected by unemployment that begins in the parent company in the neighbouring republic and the last to profit from the resources of research.

We have been denouncing the invasion of our universities by American textbooks for a long time now, particularly in Quebec. Is there any need to stress the importance of this phenomenon? A discipline does not yield up its secrets in a given language through a kind of transparency; in the social sciences especially, it is a way of seeing things, the reflection of a particular educational system, a certain general ideological climate that will set its mark on the student for ever. The war was a decisive factor in this regard, as it was for the economy. Cut off from France and England, French-Canadian and English-Canadian students had to turn towards the United States for the foreign study that normally climaxes a program of post-graduate studies. Some came back thinking that science is American and with a complete scorn for the traditions and progress of European research. This tendency has been reversed, it is true, at least among French Canadians: in some disciplines the change in attitude has been profound and study sessions in France are increasing in number. But at the same time the American influence is making itself more insidious. Publishing houses establish branches in Quebec; American textbooks are translated, most often into very dubious French. Intensive training programs are given in Quebec, in Montreal, in English Canada, and they are all controlled directly by American universities. Last year, one of the latter even proposed the establishment in French Canada of a series of courses for training kindergarten teachers.

One suspects that the American influence is more obvious and more complex in our day-to-day life. The influence of American civilization on our mores is very uneven. It is clearly felt in the mass media, but this is not a specifically Canadian phenomenon, as the Europeans know very well. In Canada more than elsewhere we must try to distinguish what comes from American culture from what is simply a sign, done up in American packaging, of the new phase of the technological civilization in which the whole world is involved. There are still parts of Canada where flourishing signs of an indigenous culture can be found. One has only to spend an evening dining in a Toronto home to see ample evidence of this and to sense the Britishness of the surroundings and attitudes. This is even more true of the French Canadians, whom I know infinitely better: just to spend a few days in a small town or in the countryside is to realize right away that a unique culture exists there and is holding its own, almost without realizing it, in its daily routine. But these traditions are threatened on all sides. They are not deep-rooted over all Canadian territory: the western part of the country (with the exception of British Columbia) is more American than English. With the revolution now going on here in the field of education and the rapid climb in the level of instruction, Quebec seems likely to become more open to the influence of American culture.

Any attempt to make a diagnosis of American hegemony soon leads back to Canada's own internal problems.

The serious deficiencies in Canadian economic policy must be brought in question. But it is necessary first of all to recognize that the context is not very favourable. American capital has not simply invaded the country. It has put at its service what we may call the economic elite of Canada. The latter is still sometimes English in day-to-day life, but its interests and ideologies are generally only the echo of American capitalism. In a number of cases this elite participates only superficially in the meetings of directors who get their basic orientation from the neighbouring country. But because of ostensibly Canadian associations, this elite helps form public opinion. No less serious is the preponderance of American labour unions in Canada: at least three-quarters of Canadian union members belong to organizations that take their orders from across the border. Not long ago, the director of an independent union expressed his concern over this question to one of the Canadians in charge of an American union affiliate. The reply was that this independence was 'an attempt to divide the labour movement and to stir up antagonism towards the Americans.'

As for the Canadian government, it has been very timid. It did try, in 1963, to intervene in the key sector of the automobile industry. The Drury plan proposed, through various customs regulations, to re-establish a balance between the export and import of automobiles and parts. The American Secretary of Commerce immediately protested and threatened reprisals. However, some progress has been made since then in the Canadian automobile industry. Some action has been taken. What is still needed is the imposition of an infinitely more severe policy. We could exercise a stronger control over foreign companies; European countries have shown how this can be done. Canada's vast natural resources, which are so attractive to foreign companies, are a powerful bargaining point. It goes without saying that further efforts have to be made to diversify the import of capital and the countries where Canadian investments are being directed. It would be necessary to go even further, following a pattern of which Quebec has already given an illustration. In order to check to some extent the flight of capital abroad, the provincial government established a pension fund that makes it possible to pull together considerable amounts of capital; in addition, the government proposed to finance independent companies in co-operation with private interests. If similar measures were intensified and combined with the import of non-American capital to finance industrial development, we might then be on the way towards a valid reaction against the economic grip of the United States. But the remedy would have to be tied irretrievably to socialist political planning. Canada is still very far from that.

It must be said that Canada does not form an integrated whole. It contains four distinct economic regions whose interests are often contradictory. The provinces are frequently in disagreement with the federal government; power is badly distributed. From the straight viewpoint of effective economic policy, Canada has to be remade.

And that is not the end of it. Culturally the country has never been so divided. For a long time now the British majority has more or less tolerated the strong French-Canadian minority. This condescension has been accompanied by day-to-day persecution: Canada has never really been the bicultural country it has at times claimed to be. The French province of Quebec, which has been engaged in a spectacular renewal for a number of years, is demanding a redefinition of its status within Confederation. Relations between it and the central government and between French and English Canadians are acutely tense. The threat of secession is felt more and more distinctly. The problem of American supremacy is presented in a new context: it is not inaccurate to say that Quebec holds the key to the future of Canada. The defenders of capitalism do not deny it. A certain French-Canadian cabinet minister in Ottawa likes reminding his compatriots of the American menace whenever they are attracted to independence. To this they are tempted to reply that the federal government has not yet been able to supply a remedy for this threat. Moreover, a good many French Canadians have very little desire to serve as hostages against the United States.

In any event, there are numerous advocates of Quebec independence who do not restrict themselves to the problems of their nation and who recognize the international scope of their position. They are looking for cultural reasons, for a fatherland, to justify their not being American. They are seeking to renew their own profound ties with France, and they devoutly hope that English Canadians will do the same for their own British heritage. There are some who understand, too, that although bonds with Europe need to be tightened, Quebec's calling, like that of the rest of Canada, is tied to the North American continent. But this is only apparently a paradox: some form of independence for Quebec is perhaps a necessary precondition for negotiation among the diverse people north of the United States who have not so far found a genuine way to co-operate and effectively check the hold of their neighbour.

One hundred years ago the Canadian Confederation was constructed in opposition to the United States. It was done hastily, with compromises that have meant that one of the partners paid too high a price. Moreover, this political structure is not adapted to present economic requirements and to the new challenges presented by our powerful neighbour. The Canadian adventure is sometimes compared to the one pursued in Europe by the countries of the Treaty of Rome. The basic intent is the same and it is a valid one. But in various ways its achievement responds to different conditions. Just as the European nations, assured of their mutual autonomy, must move more quickly towards some unified political structures, so must Canada dissolve the artificial, improvised structure that gives it apparent unity, in order to rebuild a fresh assemblage of the nations that compose it.

True it is that the roads are many and varied which lead, north of the United States, in Europe, and elsewhere, to the inevitable community of peoples.

Tasks before the nationalist

Let us stop to consider some current criticism. At first sight, our nationalist associations have no future, and this is a statement one often hears made. Until fairly recently, so the claim goes, they did excellent work, but now they are out of date. For a long time they were active in the general area of social problems; however, in the past few years a number of new organizations with specific objectives have appeared. What purpose can a national association serve in a minor supporting role? Again, like many Québécois, these associations have come to the independentist choice. There is now in existence a political party that is supposed to unite all our energies to follow this course. Why duplicate this party in

Lecture given to the Congrès des sociétés nationales du Québec (June 1970)

an association with the same objectives but less real political effectiveness?

We must get beyond these two objections. They are related to more radical questions that broaden them to include the whole issue of nationalism.

Our national associations have been stripped of the various social functions they used to perform, but so has nationalism itself. Not so long ago nationalists willingly fought to get Quebec society to be more concerned with economics. Today, nationalism is being challenged in the name of those same concerns and impugned in the name of the future as well. Do nations still have meaning in societies increasingly submitted to imperatives that flow across the old boundaries and the old national individualities? Are they not, rather, vain survivals, useless fossils that bear witness to the past while we are apparently entering the post-industrial age?

We have noted that the advent of the Parti québécois seems to rob all national associations of meaning. Yet the independentist option carries with it a far broader challenge to nationalism itself. For is independence not the completion and consequently the outgrowing of nationalism? A people submissive to largely foreign political structures cannot rely, to shore up their integrity, on a spontaneous feeling about their own identity. They must be tirelessly on the alert for ideologies and social movements that recall their reasons for going on, that rally their energies in threatening periods of history. Briefly, people in such a position need nationalism. And our own have not varied from this universal law. Yet from the moment we decide to gain independence, the old substitutes for deficient political structures cease to have any rationale, or soon will do so. 'Give us a state,' say some, 'and we will stop being nationalists.'

Nationalism and a new society, nationalism and independence: here are the two great themes we will have to keep firmly before us in our thought and action over the years to come.

For a long time nationalism was based on survival. To many people this preoccupation has overshadowed the individual importance of other values, religious ones for example, and the practical nature of certain requirements, especially in the areas of economics and politics. The nation had become the rallying point of a doctrine, of a system that took in all our great social objectives. Obsession with survival made us put together, under the cover of national concerns, 'our language, our institutions, our laws.' We had lost sight to some extent of the diversity and the dynamism peculiar to each of these areas of reality. The old synthesis is disintegrating; we want to speak French without thinking constantly of the nation to be saved; we have learned that the logic of institutions and of rights is concerned not only with ethnic groups but with social classes as well.

For some years now, we have been talking a great deal about 'neo-nationalism.' One does not have to be much of a scholar to realize that in fact today's nationalism is no longer that of the past. In many cases, especially for people in their forties, it has been defined in opposition to the old nationalism. National fervour has often reappeared as a result of other commitments, socialist ones for example. We can observe conversions of this kind every day, and they are often very astounding. The content of this neo-nationalism is still indistinct, as are the loyalties it groups together. We must clarify this in the years to come.

The first, most urgent need is to demystify the economy.

Let there be no misunderstanding. We are not opposed to bread and butter in principle, or even to a Saturday beer. And we all agree too about creating more jobs. Economic growth is obviously one of the priorities, and we have been given a very timely reminder that before we make prophecies about our post-industrial future we should first of all make certain of the development of our secondary sector. Where all that is concerned it seems to me that there is perfect agreement.

The obscurity of the economy lies elsewhere.

First of all, the term 'economy' is highly elastic. It denotes labour, capital, raw materials, markets, and many other things of the kind. But it also refers, and here we are in new territory, to general purposes, to powers that have been acquired or that are to be won, to domination and dependence. We must unravel all that just a bit, so that when people tell us about the imperatives of growth they will not try to persuade us at the same time of economic necessities in the strict sense, and of the eternal legitimacy of the powers currently profiting by them. It is a very widespread practice to place an accent on the economy which, on the pretext of necessary progress, guarantees weapons to the forces of conservatism.

Some people think it is sufficient to evoke the 'flight of investments' to silence everybody on the subject of justice or independence. Like most Québécois I condemn violence and bombs. But I am no less worried by the perverse uses the established disorder makes of terrorism. A politician declared after a bomb had exploded in Westmount, 'One thing is certain, these events are going to have an effect on investment in Quebec.' We have been hearing this for months, several times a day. Are we going to vegetate from now on beneath the terrorism of investment? We find it repugnant when our English neighbours live in fear of being blown up, but it seems no healthier to me that we have reached the point where we panic every time we see a Brinks truck at an intersection or get up in the middle of the night to scan the heavens for signs of a possible investment slump. This economic blackmail will finally wear out the last bits of that resilience that gives communities their strength and, in particular, their economic vitality. There is a possible recourse against this blackmail: a vast mass-education campaign on just those economic matters. Our businessmen who demand the teaching of more economics in the schools would agree completely with such a project. Besides, this need is not peculiar to us: in our modern societies, all responsible citizens need a high level of knowledge of this kind. It is even more necessary for the poor who have long been kept outside the decision-making processes and for whom the economy is a frightening mystery that the powerful handle with ease.

A different kind of obscurity, but one which implies the same ambiguity I have just mentioned, is the never-ending insistence on the primary importance of the economy. There are many examples of this, but I shall choose one at random. On 27 May 1969, Mr J.B. Porteous, outgoing president of the Montreal Board of Trade, addressed that organization. His remarks were reported in *Le Devoir* on May 28: 'He maintained that for a certain period of time it will be necessary to put aside any decision concerning language and education in Quebec and deal rather with boosting the province's economy.' And he went even further: 'According to Mr Porteous, we cannot consider the spread of language, religion, and culture until Quebec's economic survival has been assured.' It is a little as though you told someone you would like to see working harder that in order to do so he must forget, for the moment, the very reasons why he is working: his love for his wife and children, his faith, his highest motives for living. Would he work any harder? The same is true of communities. Does starting them on the road to progress consist in having them put aside the very values that could urge them into the paths of economic growth?

Now we are coming to the essential point. Today, confronting the problems that face all societies, even the most advanced, how do we see the basic problem of economic policy?

Let us listen for a moment to the advice of Mr Porteous and silence, temporarily, the nationalist voices. Let us listen to the greatest economists of our day. What do they say?

First, they say that the enormous resources technology has put at our disposal oblige us to make more long-term plans, taking into account a more widespread range of variables. Then, that if our means of forecasting are refined, we will be faced with choices technology by itself could not make for us. More than ever, men must formulate projects in which their values are embodied. Not only individual values, as the old liberalism of the eighteenth and nineteenth centuries would have had it, but values with a collective appeal, that represent agreement and approval by human groups on a common life-style. Will these plans and agreements penetrate the isolated consciousness by magic? Will they be the synthesis of the so-called universal values – given, as it is often claimed, that in the planetary age particularisms are nothing but an obstacle?

I am skipping over the fact that those who plead for the universal sometimes speak, in another connection, of a necessary 'Canadian nationalism,' as I want to get right down to the basic question: are nations the essential foci for working out these values, these plans required by the new varieties of technology and development? In the last analysis what we have to know is whether nationalism is the opposite of humanism or one of its indispensable component parts.

Lest I be accused of building up philosophical points that lead subtly back to my own options, I will turn to a contemporary philosopher from abroad. To my knowledge Pierre Thévenaz has never spoken of nationalism; he has reflected deeply on humanism, however, and on the rationales for its regionalization. He has wondered, for example, why the Western nations have given pride of place to the Greeks and Romans in their concept of humanity and in the education of their children. He knew that the West has been discovering in other civilizations values that are different from but just as rich as our own, and he asked why we should not combine all these values. Why continue to refer to our own particular past? Let us first hear what he says about this: 'We seem to be advancing an ideal of not stopping with any human type, of not choosing any as our own, of never shutting ourselves off in order not to lose any human possibility, of never concluding for fear of excluding. The humanist attitude can thus become an undefined curiosity, an infinite enquiry into mankind. We accumulate all the riches of humanity: are we liable to suffer from an embarrassment of riches, which is another form of interior poverty? By remaining open to all, will we not drift into a posture of dilettantism that receives humanity, greets it, samples it, but, lacking the support of a personal vocation that would be an exclusive commitment, sinks into inconsistency or breaks up in eclecticism? Does not being a man mean choosing, excluding, concluding, closing oneself to certain possibilities that are not his own; does it not mean judging, that is to say evaluating, measuring according to one's own standard?'[1]

At least, it will be said, this giddy faculty of welcoming everything excludes fanaticism. Do not those who decide on an irrevocable attachment to one particular bit of ground and its values risk being dogmatic? I do not deny it. But here is Thévenaz's next comment: 'The dogmatic intellect is one that remains unaware of its own situation in the world ... The achievement of self-awareness means consciousness of the condition or conditions one must recognize as one's own. If humanism is awareness of the human and rejection of all that is doctrinaire, we find in one single integral act, the act of awareness, both the way to all that is human and, at the same time, our situation, our firm position in relation to it ... Humanist universalism will not thus appear as the obliteration of differences between men in the name of the universal, but as the highlighting of those particular contingencies in which the universal is manifested.'[2]

In the same way, the nation is the focus and the token of an identity. It is not alone in playing this role; at another level, the West exercises it too. These particularisms are not the negation of a planetary humanism. Those who speak of 'national prejudices' are never completely wrong, but they often contribute to an obscurant mystification of the sort we detected in the economy: they confuse the closing into the self, which is a denial of the universal, with the self-awareness which is the condition of attaining it.

---

1 Pierre Thévenaz, *L'Homme et sa raison* I, 28 (1956)
2 Ibid. 35–6

This round of reflections has been quickly described. It seems to me, in any case, that in the activities of our national associations, in our work as intellectuals, in our participation in mass education, we can catch sight of some urgent duties.

My comments clearly suggest that national tasks are not and will not be exhausted by the action of an independentist party. The latter is an essential tool. But the nation is not only a political party. The values for which it acts as vehicle and which it allows to be defined reach beyond the narrow field of politics. They must be constantly recharged, with no ulterior propaganda motive, within groups, in new initiatives, in life-styles. They refer also to education and to vigilance, as nationalists have always understood before us, and that too cannot be the exclusive responsibility of a political party. Not to mention that the kinds of thinking that converge towards nationalism are diverse and that this diversity is a healthy one. The nationalism of *Action nationale* is not that of *Le Devoir*, and the latter bears little relation to some young nationalists I know. Nationalism has the indispensable functions of assembly and of dialogue which direct us in the search for an identity that underlies these fertile diversities. We have seen a solid instance of this over Bill 63 and we will no doubt have other signs before too long.

Somewhat apart from basic party strategies can be glimpsed yet more solid work to be done. I must apologize once again for sticking to a short list.

Since we have defined ourselves as Québécois a new responsibility has become ours: that of entering into a new kind of dialogue with other Québécois who are not French-speaking. In this respect, it should be unnecessary to recall that the election of 1970 was a dangerous lesson and left us a no less dangerous temptation. It brought to light a rigid division that must cause pain not only to advocates of independence but also to any man graced with a little intelligence and feeling.

We are not going to hand over our future under pressure of a blackmail that is added to and sometimes mixed with those already cited. But neither must we work in isolation. For a small people like ours, the duty of welcome and assembly is a hard one. But it must be undertaken in terms of our lives' justification, as the highest proof that liberty is turned towards others. We must look patiently for interlocutors. I think of a young Anglais who went campaigning from door to door among his compatriots for the Parti québécois. I had a long talk with him during the campaign: anything but assimilated, Anglo-Saxon to his fingertrips and prodigiously proud of the fact; anxious as well to share our values, to help construct a common home here for us all. He is certainly not unique. We must try particularly to reach the young people in our English-language colleges and universities. Not to persuade them to become faithful copies of ourselves, but to invite them to take part in our project, leaving it to them to bring their own colours and intentions.

I move on straight away to a second task. In our struggle for independence this is a traditional nationalist concern that we have quite naturally left in the shadows and which the independentists have tended to abandon to those nationalists who have remained faithful to Confederation. I am referring to our French-language brothers in the other Canadian provinces. They are already taking advantage of the new challenges we are throwing out and some of them confess it in secret. But they also feel bitterness towards us. The Estates-General showed this not long ago and, though I was not present at the sessions and was able to follow them only in the papers, I believe I understand those reactions.

Here again it is normal for a political party to urge the pace. But the nation must not be identified with a party, nor should it be confused with a state. We must start anew, beginning with our options and the present situation, to consider this old problem.

I will go even further. Even if we decide to leave Confederation we cannot be indifferent to the fate of what is at present called Canada. Our common destiny will always be closely linked, whether we want it so or not, to that of the people who surround us. We can make any hypothesis we want about the possibility of an association between Quebec and the rest of Canada: hypotheses will not take on concrete form and be translated into reality unless we erect them not only in terms of ourselves but in terms of others as well.

For nationalists, participation from now on in defining the future of the populations that live north of the United States might appear to be the most paradoxical and difficult of tasks. But on this ground too we will be able to find interlocutors. We must strain every nerve to achieve it. We think too much, perhaps, of certain defenders of federalism as it is now. The rest of Canada is not a monolith. Questions are being asked in British Columbia, the West, the Maritimes, even Ontario. The questions are obviously very diverse, but we are not the only spoilsports. To build a sovereign Quebec, and to contribute at the same time to the political restructuring of what makes up the present Canadian ensemble, are perhaps not such contradictory tasks as they seem. They are no more difficult than those that were undertaken in his time by our great predecessor Henri Bourassa.

I am well aware that these tasks have been too hastily compiled. For us, independence is the immediate task, and must be accomplished in the short term. But a people like ours will never live on calm certainties. We must continually prove to ourselves and to others that nationalism is not the introversion we are accused of and that it is simply the courageous acceptance of what we are in terms of our more universal responsibilities.

Our culture: between past and future

How can we evaluate the development of our culture during the past decade? What new challenges confront it? In connection with such questions we can only put forward here some hypotheses for reflection. Therefore I shall not draw up another balance sheet of our intellectual production over the past ten years, or even of educational reform. They have both been done often enough in books or periodicals. But I wonder to what extent, in these various attempts, we have succeeded in working out a new cultural debate. What changes have we made in the meaning of our collective utterance? Into what new dilemmas have we thus been led? Asking all these questions will remind us that when a people want to transform their culture they will soon find themselves saying things other than those proposed at the outset.

The so-called Quiet Revolution is too often alluded to chiefly in terms of its political aspects. These were important, it is true. But as is frequently the case in such circumstances, they were largely inspired by what was already happening in our cultural life. I will go even further: the Quiet Revolution was itself essentially a cultural revolution. The major economic and political changes have yet to take place.

From *Maintenant* (November 1970)

How then, in the years before 1960, did the advocates of progress, the leftists of that day, see the problem of change in our community? Broadly speaking, for them it was a matter of breaking once and for all with our traditional attitudes, developing the ability to set off in channels neighbouring peoples had taken well before we did. In the same way, it was necessary to break down the old monolithic culture and make pluralists of ourselves. Finally, and still as a corollary, we had to stop being obsessed by ideological speculation and get down to the concrete realities.

This new discussion, this new self-awareness, meant defining our collective conversion in rather formal terms. Proposing more progressive attitudes, promoting pluralism, denouncing ideologies in the name of the *concrete*: all that was not very precise in terms of the new values a changing culture had to represent. The discussion was effective, however: it gave direction to the earliest phases of the Quiet Revolution. We moved on, in various fields, to write off or to catch up. Educational reform is perhaps the most obvious illustration. Thinking of this kind was inevitable and moreover necessary to bring about a break. Yet this new cultural debate called for fresh values. Only a few reformers of the sixties have maintained their tireless advocacy of those ideals of a progress justified only in terms of formal freedom. Thus their solid statements of 1960 have become paradoxically a strange kind of abstraction.

In fact, various sectors of the population have witnessed, not an outright rejection of yesterday's arguments, but rather a profound transmutation. The themes and values of other times are still there, though in different settings: this is true whether you are looking at a Gilles Vigneault or at a René Lévesque. A bottomless rift seemed necessarily to separate the young generation of the sixties and those of past centuries. Where we might have expected the age of the prophets of reason we have seen the emergence of the 'bards' of the North Shore. Where we expected a cosmopolitan pluralism, we have seen the resurgence of the old fleur-de-lys banner, seized by young hands and waving in its thousands. Some will say that we are still repeating old forms of nostalgia. This is true in a sense. But what is its significance?

Radical breaks occurring in the history of cultures never take the form of a total winding up followed by a fresh departure. This can be verified in Quebec. In a sense – and we have often failed to recognize this – that old argument contained its own transcendence. For example, from Garneau to Groulx, from the latter to Frégault, to Séguin or Brunet, there is continuity of tradition, but also testing of an inner logic, of potential schism. There is a certain affinity between the poetry of the soil and Savard's *Menaud*, but there is also illumination from within: the masterpiece is not of another origin; it is an old story that finally, in its very despair, reveals what it had long concealed. After studying the Jesuit review *Relations* for the period from the 1940s to 1960, my students were surprised at the ease it displayed in assimilating events: the Quiet Revolution was all there in rough draft.

We could give many more examples, and further expose the criteria employed by the older consciousness in changing to survive. It may be enough to suggest that in periods of profound crisis the old debate stood for continuity while still exploring what was implicit in itself. What the old debate had kept in its depths rises again to the surface. The old problems, purposes long repressed, are seeking expression. The demonstrations against Bill 63 brought together suddenly, in the light of day, deep desires for survival that had never before related all their hope and all their despair. Many of the suggestions I heard during the sessions of the Commission on the Laity and the Church seem to me to have brought into the open what were for a long time simply private and veiled confidences. If I may be permitted an analogy with psychoanalysis, one could speak of a sort of lifting of the censorship exercised, on the surface at least, by our culture of yesteryear.

We know what the end result was. Never before have a people so long imprisoned in silence and so reticent in speech expressed themselves so fluently, in so many ways, and with such happiness. Poetry and religion came together there, passing by way of politics which itself became a kind of poetry. For better or for worse.

All that shows the limits of any really new cultural discussion a people want to hold. What, in fact, have we been doing since 1960? Was it simply a case of a minority, having survived by an oversight of history, remembering its reasons for existing? Was it the heady celebration of a society about to pass into a more silent agony? Did we produce a vocalization that would serve as ultimate alibi for the impossibility of assuming our own destiny? In fact we can no longer escape a more concentrated suffering than we have ever known in our history: despite the enthusiasm

poured into it, have the last ten years been anything more than a cultural
revolution? Are we a people who, by reason of the fatal forces at work
on us, can accomplish no more than a change in language, thus in the end
admitting the impotence already inscribed in our history?

For ten years we have been closed within the circle of culture. Our literature has gained an astonishing impetus. Young people fill the schools.
Our civil servants, frequently turning competent, keep making diagnoses
and making them well. Intellectuals abound; they are everywhere, in the
CEGEPs, the universities, newspapers, television. The people of Saint-
Jérôme and Saint-Roch, Cabano and Saint-Paulin, are beginning to talk
as well. Is this a vast classroom revolt that we have produced? For a century the word was left to us as our domain. After preserving it for a long
time, we are finally using it. But have we done no more than better explore from top to bottom the prison that was ours for so long? It may
be that we have only gone deeper into our ancestral house, this time into
rooms we abandoned a long time ago.

To look farther into the coming years, our speech and culture should
expand into other areas where at first sight they seem to have no business.
In this confined circle where we often place our culture, we are not yet
really ourselves. Even among the extreme leftists, there are accents that,
although new, are not completely local ones. We still define ourselves by
superficial comparisons. 'Colonization,' 'social design,' 'revolution' or,
in another perspective, 'social order,' 'just society,' 'economic development' – all these terms, like the French that is heard in our colleges, have
the odour of imported languages. I can see traces of it in the narrower
field of my own discipline, sociology. When we speak with young intellectuals, we often have the feeling that they are repeating, with adjust-
ment and variation, what the foreign schools and fashions have been
saying for some time. In many cases you are constantly distracted; you
look for the father behind the one speaking to you – the absent and foreign father for whom the native son on duty, previous holder of a grant
from the Canada Council or the Quebec Ministry of Education, is but
the local representative.

I do not reject foreign influences: this will be easily accepted. But our
cultural debate will have no basis unless it issues first from ourselves; if
it is defined also in terms of its effect outside the close circle of our society. For example, we talk a lot about co-ordinating research in our

universities. We should begin by ceasing to imitate what is done elsewhere
with considerably ampler means. Populous and wealthy societies dispense
culture as generously as napalm. Smaller societies are left with the re-
source of astuteness, in which noble words have a chance to fix themselves on the more profound questions that get barely a pause from the
big schemes and teams. I mean that we must commit ourselves more in
our ties with the United States and France. And we must not lose sight
of the priority of the United States. If our research does not go into the
cultural life of our neighbours as a new challenge, how can we but con-
sole ourselves with being some kind of continental relay station for
French civilization?

Reduced to its narrowest limits, our cultural problem has then become openly what it has always been implicitly: a problem of communication, in the sense however that it no longer applies to reception difficulties, but more to those of emission. Our economic problem, another
traditional one, arises from similar difficulties in communication. The
economist Jean-Luc Migue has produced some fundamental writings on
that subject. There is no more to say about the backward mentality of
our French-Canadian businessmen, in charge of small industries without
a future, torn between the desire to stay within the family circle and the
desire to give in to foreign powers, keeping only the vain glory of those
visible powers the local elites still hold in esteem. Could it be otherwise?
In every area, for two centuries, we have been cut off from channels of
communication. Are not the subsidies the federal Department of Regional Expansion gives to American businesses that want to set up shop
here not like the invitations given by intellectuals to foreign academics?
By what route will we manage to unite our tools of economic growth
and the broader decision-making processes, manage to push ourselves in
as contributors of originality in a wider arena? The question is the same
for our poetry, our fiction, our scientific research. In 1970 we are more
aware that a people, no matter how small, can only speak to make themselves better understood by others.

In Quebec a people have survived like an extraordinary paradox. Such
a paradox is not unravelled by a borrowed speech or an economic policy
copied from our neighbours. Elsewhere, the young are protesting against
the 'consumer society.' What they want to say is: 'We are protesting
against a kind of contamination of the economy and of our culture that

makes it hard to distinguish between poetry and gadgets, between improved conditions and the promotion of capitalism, between the meaning of life and the meaning of power.' In Quebec, we have been denouncing these confusions for centuries, more intensively during the past ten years, in our society itself. Will we elicit from it an original model for economic and cultural development? It seems undeniable to me that we must now put together these two aims, which have for a long time been foreign to each other. In the years to come, that will require a language where once more, this time more closely than before, the past will be mingled with the imperatives of the future.

PART THREE

Of a socialism for Quebec

The co-operative ideal

Elites and planning: at first glance, these two terms suggest an irreconcil-
able opposition. In fact, planning implies co-ordinating activities and defining long-term projects on a basis of technical criteria. The latter should
be more or less imposed on the multiplicity and incoherence of individual
wants and goals. The elite, on the contrary, represents an authority dele-
gated spontaneously by groups. The leader is not a 'good talker' or even
necessarily a 'learned man,' but he who proposes a representation of his
own milieu and objectives for action in which other men may recognize
their own viewpoint and desire for change. While planning is based on
reasoned discussion, the tasks of the elite are above all along the lines of
developing awareness. In planning, the cohesiveness of society descends
from above; we can talk about social participation by constraint. Bringing men together around common tasks, by the mediation of elites, works
from below; social participation can then be described as spontaneous.

Presented in this admittedly rough way, such an opposition constitutes
what may be the most crucial and dramatic problem that has confronted
our twentieth-century political and economic structures.

The idea of planning is not a new one. In all places and at all times,
social life has been able to operate only through some general orientation –
more or less spontaneous, more or less imposed – of the activities and desires of individuals. In traditional social milieux, this social control was
assured mainly on the level of personal relations, public rumour often
being sufficient to punish deviations from conventional modes of behaviour. Beyond that, traditions and customs suggested other ways of
acting that were protected by concrete values which were rarely questioned.

Right at the beginning of the modern era, a fissure was opened in this
type of social unanimity. Appearing first in the area of the economy, it
was mainly the work of the middle class, more precisely of the capitalist
entrepreneur. He attempted to substitute mankind's organizational drive
for the authority of customs and traditions. At the dawn of the modern
era it was he as well who invented the first calculating and forecasting
techniques: accounting, flexible banking methods, increased emphasis

Address to the Congrès des mouvements coopératifs in 1959

on practical law, and so on. He was also the one who perfected coercive systems to impose his own planning drive on society as a whole. Brandishing the charter of a democratic freedom that made everyone theoretically equal, he imposed on the worker machines that from the outset he did not want and a control, an efficiency, that made of the factory an authoritarian world. By purchasing rural properties the middle class also unleashed on the countryside the disorders that have quite accurately been termed an 'agricultural revolution.' And it was still the capitalist entrepreneur who later attempted to put unity and order into business initiatives by concentrating important powers in cartels and trusts. Finally, with production responding to its own logic, the psychological coercion of advertising has tried to shape needs to suit the decisions of business.

Through mechanisms of calculation and forecasting, and through methods of constraint, planning has been at work for a long time in our Western society. Today we are proposing to extend it into other areas: education, resources, regional economic growth, various government policies, and so on. It is only the logical continuation of a long story. Moreover, in a pluralistic society where traditions have practically no influence in bringing about unanimity among groups and individuals, planning aims must dig deeper into various facets of human existence. Thus the consummation of the old Western dream of a rational society is being carried out before our very eyes.

But we are not witnessing simply the spread of planning. Its meaning is being changed by the clear intention of changing its sources. The entrepreneur, traditional custodian of calculation, forecasting, and constraint, must gradually make room for the collectivity, working through the intermediary of the state. The state acquires new powers. Are we certain that it does so in the name of the citizens? Is it only a matter of turning over to a technocrat what formerly belonged to the entrepreneur? And more important, can the state's new policies be effective if the population itself, informed and carried along by its natural leaders, does not recognize them as the expression of its deepest desires? To express it even more directly: is the intensification of planning accompanied by a transfer of initiatives to an economic elite that is more representative of human communities?

The question is a painful one. From many points of view, one is tempted to reply in the negative. People seem less and less interested in bringing effective weight to bear on the economic or political destiny of our societies. The rate of participation in political movements, workers' organizations, or co-operatives seems rather low everywhere. We are alarmed at how hard it is to interest people in these associations, at the small attendance at meetings, at the superficial nature of the information about problems that touch people very closely.

In the various associations new tricks are thought up every day to increase the members' participation. If they have little success it is no doubt because the phenomenon is connected to some profound patterns in our contemporary society. In our complex social milieux people communicate with one another in a number of impersonal ways. Most of our information comes to us by detours that have little connection any more with conversation. Our society has used all its ingenuity to define a profusion of statuses and roles exempting us from interpersonal relationships where our personalities would be truly involved. Individuals have reacted against this anonymity in our collective life which is the source of so many frustrations. They have often found refuge in the intimacy of relationships with friends or within the family circle, or in the freedom of leisure. In contrast to what occurred in the past, private life is now opposed to public life. Mankind seeks the realization of his own highest requirements and values in a reduced area of his existence. The interior life of each one is enriched thereby, but on the other hand it has hardly any influence on the destinies of society.

These observations indicate the limitations of our traditional ways of training leaders. In mobilizing an economic elite that is equal to our current problems, it is still important, though hardly sufficient, to make individuals aware of certain problems in the context of the discussion groups that we are familiar with. More will be required: broader problems must also be brought up. As organizations grow in size it is inevitable that a large number of their members will be confined to jobs that separate them from the complexity of the social milieu.

In certain respects the current attempts at planning do offer new possibilities.

In our societies power is built up in a *vertical* manner, and we delegate authority rather than receive it. This is not only for the state, but for professional associations and no doubt co-operatives as well. For one thing, planning will certainly accentuate this process: it will no longer be possible to run democracy, as in the past, by delegating authority to continuing committees. But planning presents another dimension: that which is expressed by the term 'regional management.' This should give rise to a new organization of power which could be qualified as *horizontal*, and would complement the previous one. In this pattern a whole new form of economic democracy would be possible: people of the various regions would be able to express themselves through their local leaders. We have already had a hint of this in the regional economic councils now increasing in number in various countries and beginning to take shape in Canada.

What attitude will the co-operative movement adopt in the face of this situation, liable to bring a new economic elite into being? That is the most incisive challenge now before it. It may revive, in a very contemporary context, the old aims of its great tradition.

From the very beginning, the co-operative form of economy has had the self-imposed task of meeting concrete economic needs. Albert Thomas's remarks on this subject, made some time ago, deserve to be considered at length: 'Because the structure of the co-operative economy is based on a large number of small economic units that act as its antennae for the needs and possibilities of daily life, it has at its disposal a kind of sensory apparatus similar to that of a living organism. This apparatus is not content with transmitting by stages to the central organs information that the latter work out and translate into reasoned action; up to a certain point it also allows for automatic reactions, reflexes of defence or compensation, instructions that warn of imbalances and serious errors heavy with consequence.'[1] Is this not a magnificent definition of the special and essential role co-operative units can play in a type of planning that aims to be rational and democratic at the same time – as mechanisms for sensing regional economic needs and, at the same time, as mechanisms for correcting and controlling policies of wider scope?

That would imply an effort on the part of the co-operative movement to define new tasks, to complete difficult experiments. I am thinking of attempts to diffuse, through various sections of Quebec, economic information that was generally lacking, and of the establishment of discussion groups to consider local problems. I am thinking particularly of the po-

---

1 Speech given to the International Labour Conference, as quoted by H. Desroche in *Archives internationales de sociologie de la coopération,* 11 (1962), 9

tential for various enquiries of which the journal, *Économie et humanisme*, in France, gave many fine examples. In these investigations (where teams of volunteers, led by only a few specialists, mustered the essential research components), residents of a city or rural district had the opportunity to discover the main problems of an area of human life which, unlike those of the economist or the sociologist, had to do with the most everyday aspects of their existence. Better than all the propaganda and all the speeches, such experiments would lead to the kind of commitment that is likely to yield us new economic elites.

Originally, a main concern of the co-operative movement was to destroy the monopoly over economic initiative held by the capitalist entrepreneur. The principles defined by the pioneers of Rochdale are a perfect expression of its ideals. Their intention went considerably further than simply founding a food co-operative. In a volume published on the group's centenary G.D.H. Cole recalled: 'For Howarth and his fellow Pioneers storekeeping was but a means – one among a number of means – of forwarding the Co-operative ideal; and that ideal was the foundation of Co-operative Communities, or "Villages of Co-operation," in which the members could live together on their own land, work together in their own factories and workshops, and escape from the ills of competitive industrialism into a world – a "New Moral World" – of mutual help and social equality and brotherhood.'[2] This grandiose objective underwent much transformation and redefinition; it had to be corrected and cut down (perhaps excessively) as the movement grew in size and faced new and practical difficulties that had not been foreseen at the outset. But should not the present challenge posed by planning lead us to a broad reconsideration of the idea of a co-operative order?

The pioneers dreamed of a vast economic community that would oppose the inhumane logic of the industrial capitalism of their time. Today, when the initiative for planning is assumed to an even greater extent by the State, the co-operative movement faces the task of creating a group of economic communities capable of supplying solid and living substance for the vast technological mechanisms rising before our eyes.

2 G.D.H. Cole, *A Century of Co-operation* (1944)

The struggle against poverty

What general social changes are implied by the struggle against poverty and against social injustice in general? Leaving aside the strictly economic aspects that are dealt with elsewhere, the question could be reduced to this very generalized formula: in what way does poverty pose a challenge not only to our good intentions, our 'good deeds,' and even our politics, but to the whole of our society? At first glance, the question in this form is ambiguous. The most basic transformations cannot be guilelessly defined in terms of poverty alone. Thus poverty is in danger of being lost sight of. But I shall try specifically to show what it is that basically distinguishes the kind of poverty found in our so-called opulent societies, to see how, as in a reverse image, it challenges the entire social edifice. It is in terms of this diagnosis presented by poverty itself that I shall try to catch sight of the main outlines of future social change.

Ever since the earliest days of the true Christian tradition, a consideration of poverty has always required a dual attitude. It calls on our presence before the poor person who is on the spot and invokes immediate and concrete testimony on our part; and, on the other hand, it prompts us to contribute to the transformation of our society. The latter obligation cannot be limited to a few reforms for making poverty less odious; it implies our acceptance of the need to work towards building a society where there would be no more poor, an egalitarian and fraternal society.

A vain utopia, or so it would seem. The phrase 'society of abundance' suggests the notion that the period of widespread poverty, of poverty hitting entire groups of people, has finally come to an end. At worst, poverty would be the lot of certain regions. Otherwise it would be related to such specific causes as mental deficiency, alcoholism, lack of education, or maladjustment. Poverty would be only a relic of a condition that has been superseded by the development of collectivities, a specific problem that could be remedied by specific policies.

Recent studies of American society, the farthest along the road to affluence, completely confute this mythology.[1] Thirty-five million poor,

Address to the symposium on 'Socio-economic inequalities and poverty in Quebec' organized by the Welfare Council of Quebec, Lévis 1965
1 Conference on Economic Progress, *Poverty and Deprivation in the United States* (Washington 1962); *Economic Report of the President* (January 1964); Herman

or one-fifth of the population; 9.3 million families whose annual income
is less than three thousand dollars; 5 million single persons who receive
less than two thousand dollars annually: taken all together this is a considerable minority. Moreover poverty affects not just isolated individuals
but entire sectors and groups of the population. We know, for example,
that in the United States 40 per cent of the families who live off the land
could be considered poor: technological progress has dealt agriculture a
hard blow. Men in their forties and older have had to seek other means
of earning a living because of technological changes. There are even people who are poor as a result of planning. Alfred Sauvy has recalled the
case of those fifty thousand small businessmen whose disappearance was
envisaged by the French Fifth Plan. Other, more general, indices may be
noted: in his economic report for 1964 President Johnson emphasized
that between 1947 and 1962 the gap between the various income groups
in the United States had far from diminished.

If the poor are so numerous and yet so much effort is necessary to
show that they exist and to destroy the myth of the 'affluent society,'
no doubt this is because poverty is less noticeable now than in the past.
There used to be an actual class of poor people. Under the old regime it
was even identified with the entire labouring class. We used to talk about
the 'working classes' and the 'poor.' Today the poor are more isolated,
better hidden. The tourist rarely finds himself in the areas away from
the main highway to which rural misery is confined; we hear less talk
about poverty among old people than we do of the financial needs of
students. There are many poor people in our cities who find shelter in
neighbourhoods vacated by those who could afford to go to the suburbs,
in conformity with a process pointed out by American urban sociologists
some time ago. To point up the distinguishing feature of these new poor
people, the poor of prosperity, we could say that they are 'voiceless,' that
they lack social representation.

P. Miller, *Rich Man, Poor Man: The Distribution of Income in America* (New York:
Crowell 1964); Michael Harrington, *The Other America: Poverty in the United
States* (New York: Macmillan 1962). In French, see the excellent restatement by
Henri Perroy, 'Pauvreté aux États-Unis,' *Revue de l'action populaire* 182 (Novem-
ber 1964), 1043-57. For the situation in France, which we shall refer to in passing,
see Paul-Marie de la Gorce, *La France pauvre* (Grasset 1965).

A very similar conclusion was reached by Harrington about the United States. Perroy summarizes it in terms perfectly suited to our own society. 'In the past, when poverty was the lot of the majority, skilled and unskilled labourers, the resourceful and the retarded, those who were ready to make their way in the world and those who were waiting behind them, all the poor rubbed shoulders, lived in the same street, had a common ground for understanding or dissatisfaction. When the middle classes emerged out of the reforms of Franklin Delano Roosevelt, this community of the poor was destroyed; the disarmed fortress of the other America became a prison without bars or keepers, inhabited by those who belonged to nothing and to no one. They no longer participated in the traditions and ideals of the American Way of Life. They became less and less religious ... Those who are part of the other America are only distantly associated with unions, social organizations, and political parties. They have no formal representatives or programs of action. As they are everywhere a scattered minority, they no longer interest those seeking votes as they did when some parts of the cities were seething with immigrants or their sons.'[2]

Here we are getting to the unique quality of poverty's new sociological manifestations. It can be considered as a problem of social participation, in two complementary senses: participation in social progress, since the modern poor are not only the waste products of progress but also its ransom; and participation in defining social aims, since today's poor are even less likely than yesterday's to belong to organizations that could make their voices heard. It is thus that the process begun by modern poverty goes beyond the individual poor man and reaches the day-to-day life of every one of us: it challenges the public expression of needs and aspirations in contemporary society.

The facts that needs do not correspond to received physiological or psychological criteria and that they change as the standard of living rises are commonplaces that hardly demand repetition. More serious than this constant shifting in needs is the minimal importance given to the individual in their definition. The economy is increasingly production-oriented – and consequently the essential problem of our societies is one of consumption. We should admit to this paradox: production de-

2 Perroy, 'Pauvreté aux États-Unis,' 1046 and 1045

mands consumption; we no longer respond to the demand, we create it. Needs are no longer expressed, they are manipulated.

All this suggests extraordinary disparities between essential needs and frivolous ones, those that express the common good and those concerned with selfish private interests. Numbers and styles of cars increase, but we have not enough dwellings or green spaces. We invest huge sums to make new gadgets, but our research into the creation of jobs is still in its infancy. We produce things for those who have money to spend but in order to stimulate production we exacerbate the wants of those who cannot buy the marvels dangled before their eyes. We offer the consumer the most subtle kinds of satisfaction, but working conditions are still far from meeting the worker's most elementary requirements. In short, all things help prevent both individual and society, not only from expressing their true needs, but from giving them some kind of coherence or structure as well.

Giving structure to our aspirations and body to our collective needs: it is certainly in this light that the present forms of poverty call us to rethink our concept of society as well as the orientation of the reforms that are to be carried out. Though the modern poor person may be ill-adapted to progress and may speak out even less than the traditional poor, he incarnates the impotence of all of us; and if we attempt to transform our society to make room for him, it is for our own deliverance as well.

In this context official institutions seem to hold out the first means of reform.

The state first of all. The pursuit of the common good, for which the state is primarily responsible, comes down to a very precise objective: giving form to human aspirations. We are all increasingly aware that we have little initiative in the realm of economics and that through modern means of communication we are exposed to all kinds of persuasion. These anonymous techniques represent special interests. It is not the community which controls the advertising media that turn us into consumers of such and such a product. The state is the only collective decision-making mechanism that theoretically represents the general interest, the only one that has as its vocation the control of other social techniques and their regulation to suit our aims.

To realize how far we still are from these requirements, let us ask simply this: even if we have an educational policy and no doubt a health policy as well, where is our agricultural policy, our public-works policy, our policy for land management? One tiny example: thanks to the sales-tax rebate to municipalities, one small badly-off community had side-walks built on the outskirts of town, on both sides of the street! A striking illustration of the incapacity of our official mechanisms for defining needs.

The state is first of all a set of policies. On this point, we are begin-ning to catch up with other Western nations. But we are still far from today's real problems; not even increasing the number of these policies will do that. Think of the United States or France, countries that have preceded us on this ground. The fact that masses of poor people exist there and that, as we have emphasized, poverty is a phenomenon affect-ing the structure and the dynamic of society as a whole is a decisive test of these policies. To a large extent this test is negative. Alfred Sauvy re-cently said as much about France and perhaps his remarks could be applied equally well to the United States as to our own country: 'So-ciety has undergone many improvements; the various laws brought in are so many boxcars provided for the working world: the job car, hous-ing car, retirement car, and so on. Unfortunately, not only do these arrangements have various lacunae, but many people do not manage even to get into the train; this is the army of the maladjusted.'[3] In short, if the number of the poor and those defeated by prosperity is still so consider-able in our wealthy societies, it is primarily because a systematic set of policies has been lacking, or because those we have defined are too loose-knit, letting out too many people and too many problems. Thus we are led to make the plea for a more far-reaching, more coherent kind of planning.

But in our milieu as elsewhere, we are quick to believe in the value of planning without corresponding changes in social structures. The state, we have recalled, is the only power representing the common good and in a position to dominate other forces in society; it alone is capable of considering the true needs of all and of preventing the exclusion of so many. But how can the state become aware of needs, how can it detect

3 Alfred Sauvy, 'Les ombres de la France riche,' *Le Nouvel Observateur*, 24 June 1965

those defeated by prosperity? Although the state has at its command the enormous powers implied by true planning – the kind we are asking for – is it not too massive and distant to be a good detection device for the aspirations of men and various groups?

Just below the level of the state, but still within the official sphere of the life of society, are those representative associations which, in the past few years, we have been so willing to see as the most appropriate vehicles for expressing society's opinions and needs. For the moment, the role of these associations appears necessary and, in any event, unavoidable. But considerations of poverty and social inequality have put us on the road of radical evaluation of our social mechanisms; so we continue in this direction, wondering how these associations can claim to express the aspirations of their members and to define a collective ideal.

How is the recruiting of these associations carried out? Is it simply a question of a list of names written down in a register, as is the case for a number of associations that used to speak out so readily in the name of Catholics or French Canadians? A remark by Michel Van Schendel, concerning the recent convention of the *Caisses populaires*, gives an example that is precise and informative: 'The working-class population of the cities forms 65% of the urban population. It supplies 70% of the members of the urban *Caisses populaires*, but only 29% representation in their administration. In fact, the administrators and professionals who make up only 28% of the urban population occupy half the seats. In the country the reversal of proportions is even more flagrant.'[4] We might ask whether the associations give adequate expression to their constituents' opinions. Some highly interesting studies carried out in the United States should be noted here. Under the Roosevelt administration, for example, a big association of milk producers protested, in the name of its members, against a government decision. The government held an inquiry, asking the members of the association for their own opinion: this was shown to be against the official declarations of the association that claimed to represent them. Many similar cases could be cited.

If we wish to examine how much associations can contribute to the definition of a collective ideal, we must clearly ask how representative

4 Michel Van Schendel, 'La paroisse contre le peuple,' *Le Magazine Maclean* (August 1965)

they are, not only of their members, but of the whole of society. Does not a given association draw its strength from its control of publicity media that is disproportionate sometimes to the number and importance of its membership? And what is the respective weight of these associations? One sector of society can be very well organized while another is completely disorganized, although still exercising a strong influence on the policies of the state. The poor, despite their numbers, are not represented by any associations. They are part neither of a chamber of commerce nor of a trade union. They do not participate in any synthesis of the common good which is simply the coalition of special interests, even if the latter were all represented by organized groups. The example of countries where associations play an official role, as in the French Economic Council, is a clear indication of this. Temporary coalitions are formed to get adoption of a measure favourable to a group on condition that the favour is returned the next time, when a new alliance will promote the interest of another group. It is hard to see how such jobbery could result in a collective ideal. In any case, the poor would be bound to pay the shot.

Representative associations thus rarely make a decisive contribution to solving the problems we have raised. This is because they are already on the side of the state, whether or not they are consecrated as official tools; they assume the same abstract structuring of human aspirations. Unlike the state, they cannot claim to bring out an overall view of social needs. It may be asked whether recourse to associations is not, for the state, a means of comforting public opinion, that vague, superficial, and changeable collective awareness. Possibly the state must be satisfied with this recourse for the moment. But it must realize that it is supporting a shaky edifice and that the opinions of the citizens, particularly the poor, are not expressed in it. The state should look farther afield, into the core of society, for evidence of the aspirations and ideals of the collectivity.

If we try to go beyond these official social mechanisms that claim to express the common will, we reach men's attitudes and their varied situations – not those of every individual, but of those who have some influence on the destiny of groups, that is to say the social elites. Their leadership consists in defining social situations so as to bring together a certain number of people: it is, then, the composition of our elites and the legitimacy of their power that we should examine.

Individuals find themselves at unequal distances in relation to values recognized by the community: money, education, prestige, power, and so on. Classes imply different ways of participating in these values. These enormous groups are no longer automatically represented by associations, as was the case before the French Revolution; in the proliferation and crisscrossing of factions that bring official pressure to bear on the state today, we are well aware that in the last analysis it is not the lower classes, it is not the poor, who have the most spokesmen. The bourgeoisie, particularly the capitalist entrepreneurs, have defined our Western society. They worked out the first ideology of democratic equality according to which all are equal under the law and have only to get on with their personal ascent of the social ladder, leaving the lazy and less gifted clinging to the lower rungs.

Like all Western societies, French Canada has submitted to the definition of collective needs and ideals brought forward by the capitalist elite. But it is not absolutely necessary to fall into plaintive nationalism to remember that this capitalist elite hardly flourished on French-Canadian soil. In 1831, during a visit to Canada, Alexis de Tocqueville wrote in his notebook: 'It is easy to see that the French are the conquered people. For the most part the wealthy classes belong to the English race ... The commercial enterprises are virtually all in their hands. They are truly the ruling class of Canada.'[5] We have lived in a society that in terms of economic needs and objectives, in terms of wealth and poverty, we have never defined.

We are not surprised, then, that our native elites should have conceived an ideal for our society whose reference was outside North American economic life. The game of politics assumed the function of social awareness. Remember the vigorous and ironic remarks of Edmond de Nevers in 1896: 'One thing alone flourishes and prospers in the province of Quebec, in progressive centres as well as in the small towns of diminishing population. The French-Canadian people devote themselves in delight to one sport (which, for a certain number, could be called an industry) – politics ... In the province of Quebec (population 1,300,000), the 70 federal members, 73 members of the local legislature, their 143 adversaries (themselves would-be representatives), the 24 senators, 24 legisla-

5 Alexis de Tocqueville, *Oeuvres complètes* (1957), V, 210

tive councillors (provincial senators); the 200 or 300 young people who dream of future glories as members of parliament and are preparing for such a career, carefully studying the scandalous party records; the MPs' clients, aspiring to posts in the public administration – these devotees of politics make up almost the entire intellectual resources of the French race in Canada.'[6] Let us add: almost all of its elites.

At present our society is facing crucial decisions. Are we going to opt for independence or for a renewed federalism? Shall we push planning further ahead or are we going to be content with the timid attempts of recent years? Are we going to endow ourselves with the renewed values that could achieve some unanimity despite our differences, or be satisfied with the hardware that is characterized vaguely as 'pluralism'? All these questions are important, but sometimes I think they bring us to a more fundamental question. Beneath the social changes now affecting us there is one that presupposes them all: that of our elites. It is beginning to be very clear that our traditional elites are in mid-crisis. A new kind of political man, still uncommon it is true, is beginning to challenge the model we have grown used to. The man from the liberal professions has lost much of his prestige; at any rate he is no longer alone in expressing ideals and values. Our petite bourgeoisie is timidly seeking fresh justification; the crisis about the chambers of commerce made this clear to everyone. Finally, the new elites (particularly active members of workers' and cooperative movements), after working for a long time in the shadows, may be about to take their turn claiming the floor.

These rearrangements will force us to consider brand new options. If we want the needs of our society expressed, and if we want a collective ideal worked out that does not represent a radical break with our past, our choice should be clear: we must support the new elites. They have a greater chance of expressing the will of the poor; they are also the ones who best incarnate the ideal of an egalitarian society.

But these new elites will constantly be tempted to give in to traditional modes of social upgrading, or to look on the various badges conferred on them by their active involvement as a subtle means of 'arriving.' There must be a counterweight to these temptations. The new elites will define

6 Edmond de Nevers, *L'Avenir du peuple canadien-français* (1896, new edition 1964), 90, 104-5

our society only if they can find, in a co-ordinating ideology, the seat of solidarity and the vision of a new social order. I am not talking about a ready-made ideology that will descend from some kind of literary Sinai. It should rather be a combination of themes and viewpoints liable to take root in our attitudes, to draw sustenance from the best in our ideological traditions, to catch up with the forms of social organization already at work among us.

So we come to the last level of the social fact that is being challenged by contemporary forms of poverty. If the affluent societies have shut so many out, if they have produced so many new-style poor, might this not be because the ideal of growth and prosperity is inadequate?

I suspect a certain naivety in President Johnson's 1964 announcement of an anti-poverty law. Its purpose, he said, was to build 'an America where *every citizen* shares in all the advantages of his society, where *every man* has the chance to raise the level of his own well-being to the limits of his potential.' Is this not precisely the same vague ideal that has long served as an alibi for those who have profited from the general prosperity? Is it not the same ideal that has restricted so many members of the American middle class to the pursuit of their own narrow personal advancement? This is why the American war on poverty is limited largely to palliatives: relief for unemployed young people, appeals to groups and citizens to decide on local projects to which the federal government can give financial support, health care, aid in developing basic education and so on. These things are not to be disparaged, but they do little to illuminate the deep sources of the disease that are to be found in social institutions as a whole and in the broad ideal that inspires the American people.

Policies that are multifarious and minutely defined could hardly achieve any kind of abstract synthesis of 'functional politics.' Long-term planning implies choices of common goals and values, but here again it is hard for me to see how the state alone could conceive these goals and values without the description of a collective ideal coming to it from society. President de Gaulle's *politique de grandeur*, President Johnson's formal democracy, the centre-left stand of Mr Lesage, the Fulton-Favreau formula, the choice of Canada or separatism – all these could not add up to a constant ideal. If the discussions thus opened are not vain, they refer in any case to more concrete collective ideals. Men, especially poor men, want more than a prosperous society. They desire a fraternal society where they can share not merely the fruits of economic growth but an ideal as well. It is surprising sometimes to see today's revolutionaries mixing poetry and economics, protesting against sexual taboos and pleading for social planning. We would be mistaken to see in this formless magma mere confusion of minds and types: among many other indications I note the feeling that society is not an apparatus for the division of labour, one that has to be brought still nearer perfection, but that it is also, and above all, the scene of a collective purpose in which people want to be committed along with all their own values.

It should be stressed at the outset that a collective ideal is not invented like a specific policy. A society cannot formulate such an ideal without a certain continuity with relation to the values of its own past. There is an analogy here with the situation of an individual: whatever radical conversion of himself and his conception of the world he may glimpse at some point in his existence, the individual cannot wipe out his past at one blow. A collectivity that is forced to a radical redefinition, as is the case at present in French Canada, must find in the reinterpretation of its history the continuity of its original nature and some suggestions for future tasks. These dreams of the past continue to inspire, not only ideologists or students, but also those working in more obscure situations to transform our milieu. If the CNTU differs from the other American trade unions and is often an object of admiration for leftists, it is because it has pushed up out of this ancient soil. Should we not say the same of our co-operative movement and even of our fervour for education? In the first results of some research we are carrying out at Laval on union leaders, which is to be widened to include leaders of the co-operative movement, it was striking to note how these men are marked by our traditional ideologies, to what extent they have already, gradually, transmuted the old ideals into the form of a destiny. In several of their long autobiographical accounts, one notes the evolution through the Jeunesse Ouvrière Catholique of the 1940s, through themes taken from a kind of Catholicism that was unsophisticated but had defined its basic loyalties, to some elements of a nationalism that was not that of the politician who held sway not so very long ago in the name of usurped values.[7]

---

7 As an introduction to the subject see the thesis by Claude Beauchamp of the Department of Sociology and Anthropology of Laval University on trade union mili-

Is it not now our duty to bring out into the full light of day this still very confused transposition of traditional values into values of the future? Personally, I do not accept the hasty polemical surveys that have been offered to us in the past few years on the subject of our old ideologies. In opposition to that mass of politicians, aspiring politicians, and politicians' valets whom we have long been railing against in this country, we must recognize that there existed a minority of journalists, civil servants, members of the clergy, and even some politicians. In every generation since 1850 these men have denounced the frivolities of politics. They often misunderstood the requirements of the economy or, when they did perceive them, noticed only the Anglo-Saxons' quasi-exclusive hold on the machinery of control. We find them a little ridiculous for so often singing the praises of agriculture, but for some of them that was a solution born of despair. In particular, and this is the lesson we must be careful to retain, they were very attentive to the fate of the poor and the powerless. Their denunciation of industrialization and their exaltation of rural life were profoundly motivated by that concern. And that too is what led them to conceive the dream of an egalitarian society. I have tried elsewhere to recreate this dream and I hope to return to it at length in another work.[8] I shall confine myself to one example. Here is a text written by Henri Bourassa in 1919: 'Let there be no mistake – the material prosperity and economic resilience of the French-Canadian people do not depend upon the acquisition of large individual fortunes by means of English and American methods, but on the normal growth, constant and general, of the national heritage through the practice of indigenous virtues inherited from France. One hundred habitants, each of whom saves a hundred dollars a year, are worth infintely more to the province of Quebec than ten businessmen each of whom realizes an annual profit of a thousand dollars. The sums are equal: the economic and social value of the first is worth ten times as much to the collectivity as the second.'[9] I could cite many similar references. We find there, as will

tants of the working class. The lengthy autobiographies the author has gathered reveal how the militants found in traditional ideologies, in the Jeunesse Ouvrière Catholique, for example, the first and lasting stirrings of left-wing thought.

8 Fernand Dumont, 'La représentation idéologique des classes au Canada français,' *Cahiers internationaux de sociologie* XXXVIII (1965), 85-99

9 Henri Bourassa, *Syndicats nationaux ou internationaux?* (a collection of articles from *Le Devoir*) (1919), 42 and 16

have been noted, a curious lack of realism in relation to the conditions of overall economic growth and the very fine ideal of a society in which all would participate equally in social progress.

I shall perhaps be criticized for reviving these old ideas when the question is to settle the conditions for an urgent war on the causes of poverty. I have indulged in this historical reminder because it points up a valid heritage where our collective evolution could find its needed continuity – on condition, of course, that this ideal past can be transmuted into visions of the future which, while taking it up, locate it at the same time in a broader ideological context. I believe I can find this latter in the old aims of the great co-operative tradition. We must be careful here. I am thinking less of the strictly economic bearing of the co-operative movement than its value as a representative of social ideals. For me, this objective links up with our past dreams of an egalitarian society, and moreover it seems to me that it suits a society like ours which has never known either the temptations of great wealth or a large capitalist bourgeoisie. Besides, co-operative thinking can resolve the problem we have constantly stated: expressing the concrete economic needs of everyone and every region. A long time ago Albert Thomas defined co-operation as the instrument *par excellence* for perceiving needs: that is, in fact, the special and essential role co-operative units could play in a planning activity that would attempt to be global and democratic together, as well as loyal to the principle of taking the needs of everyone into consideration in a society where participation would no longer be the privilege of a few.

I am well aware that this objective is still only vaguely defined. It is not up to the sociologist or the philosopher to define concrete and precise ideologies: that is really the role of the social elites who are elites, in fact, simply because of their ability to identify objectives in which all may recognize their most valid hopes. It is for this reason that I have taken the consideration of poverty as the departure point for a look at the whole body of our social problems. I believe I have shown that poverty, in the midst of our rich societies, raised first of all the problem of social participation: we cannot think of extending the benefits of economic progress to the poor without at the same time giving them a means to express themselves, and without examining the basic terms of a new society in which all could express their needs and commune through an ideal brotherhood. Poverty poses a test to our good conscience and we must try to understand all its reactions.

Our forefathers used to talk about the 'high dignity of the poor in the Church of Jesus Christ.' For them, it was the poor man, feeling more than others the profound sense of the evangelical community, who guided all the faithful into admittance to the mystery of the Christian fraternity. That is an idea which could also be taken in a profane context. The poor man is the reverse image of the ideal society. He can cause each of us, in our efforts to understand and transform our societies, to go beyond such limited systematic practices as little soothing reforms, and such careful abstractions as vicarious revolution.

Socialism is utopia

That socialism is utopia is quite obvious. It is so for very realistic reasons – because it does not want to abandon the collective future to the interplay of blind forces or interests; because there is no other way in which a society can gain some little ascendancy over its situation than by projecting itself into a full and solid image of its future. Thus political choices are not dependent only on disparate sets of circumstances and surface compromises, but also find coherence and perspective in more clearly fixed alternatives.

Our contemporary societies have never needed utopia so badly. The growing use of planning, no longer advocated just by socialists, calls for basic long-term choices: these choices must be something more than a scattering of abstract statements about the promotion of well-being, abundance, expansion of leisure, or even education for all. Well-being for what, abundance of what, leisure to do what, education to give access to what collective values? Only an appropriately utopian thinking can give some specific content to our anticipation and selection. Besides, the ideals our old liberal societies lived by are on their last legs: quite apart from the belief in formal and abstract freedoms, uncertainty and disenchantment are spreading. The fact that one has to be a millionaire to have any important place in the democratic mechanisms of our American neighbour is adequate proof of the realistic approach taken by those who look to utopias by way of replacement.

This paper and the next make up an address to a symposium on socialism organized by the social science students of the University of Montreal (February 1967).

Socialism is not only a utopia trying to take concrete form. It declares that all citizens should make some contribution to determining the goals of society. This places the intellectual's role in prophesying the future within fairly strict limits. Our role is essentially critical, so long as we interpret that word very broadly and with due regard for all its subtleties. We can only keep coming back to the general thinking with a militant action that ought to carry on at its own risk and peril, but which threatens constantly to be bogged down in inconclusive combat and the whole jumble of events. In other words, we can only issue reminders of the guidelines of the socialist tradition and show how this tradition sheds light on today's tasks and how it can draw nourishment from them for its own development.

This idea of a socialist tradition is an important one, for several reasons that help to define its content and how to make use of it in the French-Canadian context. First there are the terms of dialogue: our socialist loyalties are varied and in fact socialism has always been many-faceted. I see this as indicating genuineness, as evidence that the freedom we anticipate for the future exists already in our present struggle. On the other hand, the reference to this tradition is a touchstone, particularly in Quebec's present situation: our socialism has almost no home-grown past and it could bring together the oddest assortment of movements in opposition or revolt, all the ills of bad conscience veiled by a few Marxist allusions. There is no advantage to our socialism, while it is still young, in tapping these reservoirs of childishness, and we must never cease to judge it by the tradition whose heirs we would like to be. Finally, the tradition is our guarantee of the utopia, the soil it feeds on, the proof that we are not projecting fitful dreamings into the future: our hopes have existed for centuries in Western society as its constant remorse, and generations before us have taken them as a rule of life.

Can we boil this tradition down to its essential elements? In the nineteenth century, socialism was grappling with one of the fundamental characteristics of modern Western society: the monopoly of one social class in the decision-making process. Socialism began as a critique of power. But what it was challenging behind the power was a culture. This word culture should be understood with all its ramifications: a totality of collective values, of ways of thinking and determining the ideas of society, and, most importantly, a way of living together. For socialism has never dissociated culture from the daily relationships between men or dissociated them from power. It would not be difficult to show conversely that such separations are the distinctive mark of bourgeois civilization.

Nineteenth-century socialists translated the struggle between power and culture into a challenge to the bourgeoisie. That class was the concrete manifestation of the monopoly of economic and political decision-making; it also represented a type of culture whose borders were clearly drawn in relation to the people's attitudes and life styles. The socialist utopia could then be worked out on the basis of a distinct pattern: the bourgeoisie was its contrary, and popular traditions, still alive in the urban milieu, its support.

If we retain the basic aims of nineteenth-century socialism, they cannot avoid taking a very different form when we translate them into the social context of today.

The traditional work patterns of the various trades have been dissolved by the organization of labour in terms of efficiency criteria, a process which long ago reached even the white-collar workers. Allegiance to a company tends to replace attachment to the customs and rites of trades or professions. The income spectrum incorporates a greater diversity; mass consumption has given at least an apparent continuity to standards of living. Life-styles are no longer in themselves aligned on one side or another of definite borders; they are no longer subcultures. They differentiate among themselves, not with reference to different inherited forms of behaviour but rather according to a variety of entangled criteria: type and area of residence, occupation, income, and so forth. These are fragile referents for establishing differentiation between individuals, in a social world in which symbols of identity no longer form a coherent system.

In short, it is not possible to delimit, as precisely as in the nineteenth century, a society in which socialism is attempting to offer the alternative. Class lines are far more fluid than in the past; they do not coincide with power confrontations or with confrontations in clearly defined life-styles. Does this mean the problem has vanished? Far from it: it has shifted, and it is this that calls for evaluation.

The old ties between power and property have largely been broken. This is so obvious there is no need for further comment on it. The true power-holders are usually those chosen by property owners: in many cases they are even wage-earners. An analogous observation could be made of political power. Let us simply record these truisms, but note at the same time that the old analyses supplied by socialism still have currency. Although the dichotomy between property owners and non-property owners, between bourgeois and proletariat, is less obvious than it used to be, the dichotomy between power and social participation is still as marked.

The structure of power has changed and our challenges to it should be changed too, but the relation between power and culture has altered as well. Because of their social context, nineteenth-century socialists accorded a kind of primacy to the challenging of power; we should devote ourselves instead to the testing of culture. I am not unaware that this statement may seem abrupt and disconcerting, and so I shall illustrate it with a very specific example. Our socialist antecedents rebelled against the absolute opposition between bourgeois and popular culture. They were moved to this by the strict separation in life-styles; school attendance by the children of the people was so limited that so-called humanist culture appeared at once as the symbolic representation of class privilege. The problem has changed profoundly and this is cause for rejoicing: the daily life of the people and of the bourgeoisie are intermingled; advertising broadcasts the same values to both. It would be fairly shabby to continue the socialist tradition by struggling now for the objective of a car for every man, a mink coat for every woman, or 'professional' status for the majority.

Besides, the modern bourgeoisie has sanctified the separation of private life and the world of politics. There is no strict relationship between labour and what it implies as a way of existence, and evenings devoted to subjectivity. Values are potted plants whose care and feeding we study in school, and to which, in principle, we devote part of our leisure as adults. Culture is an ingredient or a trade: it apparently has nothing to do with the chain of events in which every day most men, educated or not, must get involved to earn their living or their prestige. For a contemporary socialist as for those of other times, it is a matter of knowing whether a culture is truly distinct from power or if, on the contrary, it is culture only because of a certain power. The question is clearer and more decisive than in the nineteenth century. Bourgeois culture is sold at the corner store or the local university; as it becomes detached from property, power realizes what its essence is infinitely better than it did a hundred years ago: its rationality and its systematization, which are at the same time its challenge and its appeal to collective values.

Concentrating decisions, bureaucracy, and technocracy stripped the nineteenth-century bourgeoisie of their claim to designate the reason for decisions and at the same time the values that were supposed to support them. Power appears in all its nakedness; culture as well. Both have pursued their separate destiny sufficiently to enable us to perceive the problem of their relationship. In every way, power today comes down to planning: that is, to determining the technical conditions by which values may be selected. Power invites a culture that is more than a return engagement for historical disappointment, or compensation for daily work – a way of living, and of defining finalities, and the destiny of mankind. The decline of classical capitalism and the clearer emergence, beyond the abstract opposition of economic regimes, of basic questioning of the technological society, allow us to offer again in its new form, but at the same time in a sense that is profoundly faithful, the age-old question of socialism.

Socialism for Quebec

We all know how the problem of economic power is traditionally looked at in our milieu. As we have never had a substantial bourgeoisie of our own, and control almost none of the big machinery of capitalist growth, our ideas on these lines could only sway between the contestation of the modern economy in the abstract, and claims launched in the name of the national collectivity. Inevitably the class struggle has escaped us, all the more so as the economic powers that could have been challenged by our working class were, because of the nationality of the holders of power, outside our society. We contented ourselves with demanding more room for French Canadians in business, the development by 'our own people' of a native industry and commerce. There was solidarity between our petite bourgeoisie and the people facing a power that appeared first as foreign before it was shown to be capitalist.

Over several decades the outline of the problem has altered slightly. Because the state has become more important in our collective life, economic power is revealed more clearly. We measure our inferiority less in terms of ethnic participation in big business than in terms of social development. Learning that the taxable income of Quebec is approximately half that of Ontario, more and more French Canadians begin to question not so much the absence of a large economic bourgeoisie as the various mechanisms of an under-developed society. Superficial though this change in perspective may be, it is the basis for building our own socialist society.

Implicitly at least, our national petite bourgeoisie is thus losing its traditional justification. We are no longer hypnotized by its ancient inferiority, and we do not see very clearly where, in the coming attempt to escape our collective poverty, its leadership role might lie. We see it confusedly as a simple by-product of that poverty. One task of our brand of socialism is to expose it constantly so the entire population can see it, so as to bar the way for any change in the goals of this bourgeoisie.

For the danger of a resurgence of the ascendancy of this small native elite is not an illusory one. The change in perspective on economic power and the reinforcement of political power have brought about a transformation in bourgeois strategy. As far as I am concerned I see this as a striking example of the ideology of 'representative associations' that is now fashionable. I shall not repeat the criticisms of the political foundation of this ideology: that is easy to do. I shall limit myself to emphasizing the danger it holds for the still fragile power of the state in Quebec. Moreover it helps maintain a superficial idea of 'social participation' at the very moment when this expression is being worked to death. It gives the impression that the entire population is helping to develop the aims of the collectivity and, even more insidiously, that official social power corresponds to hidden powers. Here is a second task for socialism in the years to come: the techniques of these representative associations must be exposed, including how they recruit membership and how they make decisions. That is a key point on which socialist criticism could show where there is rift and where there is continuity between the population and the new social powers.

Powers are becoming fluid. Their meaning is continually changing. This is easily observed in all Western countries, but perhaps it is more striking here. Consider the trade union movement, to take the most obvious example. No one would deny that the massive admission of white-collar workers and the appearance of 'professional' unions have changed

the movement's meaning somewhat. Nor, at first glance, do we confuse teachers' strikes with those of textile workers. This constant re-
evaluation is needed: it too is one of the new tasks before socialists in
Quebec.

If I make a plea for criticism, it is not because of any kind of intellectual mania. Socialism is first of all an interrogation of the whole of society. It is by means of overall criticism that our struggles may avoid
bogging down in circumstance or limited reformism. The socialist critique also implies a choice among all the bases available to the interests
and aims of the groups present on the social chess-board, a wager on a
power that can allow us, more or less provisionally, to unravel the ambiguity of the future. In Quebec's present circumstance, the first necessity is to opt for the state. Like everybody else, I see deficiencies there;
the play of political parties holds little enchantment for me. Yet I have
not failed to observe, again like everybody else, a basic continuity between the parties that have come to power over the past few years; this
continuity is less that of the parties than that of the apparatus of technocracy already in office. It is ridiculous to say, as is often done, that
technocracy is a danger for Quebec because it is supposed to operate
from some sort of criteria that are exclusively scientific. Such an assertion is debatable, moreover, for all the Western countries. Our young,
frail technocracy is one of the only decision-making groups to embody
a fairly precise idea of the general good. For a long time we have put up
with a sentimental coalition of small interests: it is time that some large
imperatives, economic ones particularly, were set before us in all their
severity. I still do not see that as socialism; because of its tradition, socialism is not sympathetic to the state. But let us not burn our bridges.
Think of today's duties in the light of tomorrow's. With this viewpoint,
we must do all we can to see that the State of Quebec emerges amid our
various confusions as the key power. The prime imperatives can be seen
in this light, that is the outline of that trough of pseudo-prosperity at
whose edge the most diverse interests shuffle implacably – at times in the
name of the left. It is from this viewpoint also that our age-old quarrel
with Ottawa acquires its primary meaning: beyond the proletarian condition of our nation, it becomes a question of whether the state should
not be tailored to the society whose under-development and desire for
growth it represents. Independentism would thus find its surest path,

just between the solid daily humiliations of French Canadians and the reassuring and abstract generalities of federal pseudo-planning.

To sum up, socialism should support everything that can induce a settlement of the ambiguous aspects of our situation. Since the beginning of the Quiet Revolution, opinion here has been essentially changeable. As everything has been subject to re-evaluation, it all assumes the air of the left and – here we must be careful – of socialism. We are being dragged towards questionable struggles. It is most urgent that we separate the obsession with change from the old aims of socialism. It is most urgent that we bring all the interests face to face, and oblige the groups to define themselves in terms of long-term objectives and sacrifices. To all the arguments around in favour of planning may be added a few that are peculiar to ourselves: we are a people who have been poor and suffering for centuries, now shuttled endlessly from one ideological explanation to another, and planning alone can give us an arena for collective debate on the building of our future.

For us, this is how to achieve the liaison, traditional in the socialist purpose, between the challenge of the power structure and the testing and tempering of the culture. I have remarked that socialism refuses to consider culture as the play of the solitary consciousness; it sees it first in daily life and in social relations whose genuineness it aims to restore. It does not dissociate the living culture from the common setting of social goals. If we challenge the powers of the economy and our traditional elites, it is because they do not represent a true and universal participation, and because they fail to define the future of the human community. Planning is a means of denouncing interests and oppressions masked as liberalism, and of bringing about the emergence of new social elites for which today's young technocracy can be only a temporary substitute.

The whole business of training active socialists is here under examination. Do not look at it first in terms of the limited objective of a training school, although that is indispensable. These men must not only be educated in economic machinery and socialist strategy: much more profoundly, they must incarnate in thought and action the ideals of a new culture, the foretaste of the mores and values of the socialist world. Consider the dilemma of the party member from this point of view. One of my former students put it well in his thesis: 'As a worker, the militant expresses his solidarity with the working class, but enjoys a special status and feels himself to be a member of a working-class elite. In accordance with his faith in a collective solution for the workers' problem, he will opt for the struggle of the entire working class.' Moreover 'he will sacrifice his working-class solidarity if his special status within that class allows him to glimpse an individual solution to the achievement of his aims, particularly if no collective solution is proposed to him.'[1] In other words, the working-class member is confronted not only with powers that he must defy and lead others to challenge: in his own activity, and in the status he gains through it, he is involved in the aspirations of the society around him. The road is lit only by foreign values and a foreign culture. In this very specific context, we realize again that the significance of socialism's work is indissolubly cultural as well as political. The new militant elites will not truly define our society unless they can find, in a co-ordinating ideology, the ground for solidarity and the vision of a new social order.

We cannot produce this ideology entirely in a few intellectual coteries: that might help us to mobilize people, but it would contradict the idea of cultural rootedness and integrity that socialism is always reminding us of. Let us note two dangers that await us in the current state of our society, and which socialism owes it to itself to point out.

First there is the intemperate use of the word 'pluralism.' We can only congratulate ourselves for having got out of the ideological intolerance of former times. But we cannot accept that we must be satisfied from now on with a kind of ideological hardware whose liberty would be as empty as it would be absolute; for that would mean leaving the whole field, basically, to individualistic freedoms, and, as all societies make some kind of image of the future for themselves, we would have no choice but to fall back on the insipid reverie of abundance. From the same viewpoint, we must also denounce our habitual illusion of the *tabula rasa*: we all think we start spontaneously from zero with respect to past generations. That is a paradoxical way to try to convert a culture to socialism, one that would involve a radical break with that culture in order to ask it afterwards to see itself in the ideal being presented. I am sure that this was not the procedure followed by our socialist ancestors:

---

1 Jacques Godbout, 'Le militant syndical de la CSN,' thesis in sociology, Faculty of Social Science, Laval University (1965), 187

they were concerned, Marx as much as the others, to read history that could show the continuation of certain past aims in relation to their own. We must ourselves agree to a similar effort to recuperate our historical tradition.

To my mind, this is the most important task in the building of socialism in Quebec. The point is clearly not to let the old ideologies continue in their self-appointed course. Catholicism used to play the part of framework in our social tradition. It acted also, in a profoundly ambiguous way, as the base for criticism of capitalist society and also as the justification for our submission to its imperatives. It is a very good thing that Catholicism can no longer play such a role; as a believer, I am delighted to see that the faith is no longer the miserable crutch of an under-developed society. We must not turn back to the terms of the ideologies of yesterday and long ago, but rather to the issues that gave birth to them and the utopian nostalgia they express. On the one hand, we have to redeem the long and terrible anguish that runs through our history and acted as a perpetual appeal to a sense of community life. Few societies have experienced these questionings as we have; few collectivities have felt as deeply as our own that there is no profound support for human relations but a utopia. On the other hand, having run up increasingly against economic limitations and cultural exploitation, our society has written into its past ideologies not only conservative themes but, even more fundamentally, the patiently reiterated dream of an egalitarian society. Glancing through the works of our writers, we see the statement of this ideal on every page.

To resume our ties with this bygone sensibility would mean, in terms of our socialism, opening up for ourselves our own authentic, historical existence. At the same time, it would show that for a society long tormented by the precariousness of its situation and the powerless awareness of its exploitation, there is no continuity in its destiny, no image of its future, but in socialism.

What is a political program?

Our society may be working out a serious kind of political thinking, but we are still groping, as it is particularly difficult to relate together such disparate requirements as our economic weakness and our desire for independence, our democratic aspirations and our socialist inclinations. These difficulties are reflected in the program of the Parti québécois. Not surprisingly, it gives rise to a type of thinking that, though committed, is still critical. Combining political conviction and free inquiry, unconnected with election-time manoeuvring, is no doubt one indication among others that things can change in Quebec's political life.

We are hardly in the habit of taking political programs seriously. With a few rare exceptions, they have simply been pretexts. Our traditional parties are organized for their clienteles. Immediate circumstances or habits determine how we vote. At times special interests attract us to the parties. Their ideologies are related to very general themes, lacking the power to put together any concrete imperatives or give them full freedom to manoeuvre according to variations in public opinion. 'Autonomy,' 'prosperity for Quebec,' 'constitutional revisions,' 'a strong Quebec in a strong Canada,' 'equality or independence,' 'a new Quebec,' 'a just society – none of these really constitute a program or incite critical analysis. We are faced with teams put together to take over the political machine and we do well to judge them first by their personnel. The parties themselves are probably right to tell us, when we object to some piece of legislation, 'If you don't like us you can throw us out at the next election,' but they have on some recent occasions claimed that if we do not agree with those elected by the people we should get ourselves elected in the next campaign. They say politics is for everybody, on condition that we do not get too far from the ballot box and its ritual. It can thus be advanced that democracy has been safeguarded and, in one sense, this claim is not completely wrong.

These general thoughts formed the preface to a special issue of *Maintenant* in March 1970 devoted to the program of the Parti québécois. They are included here only as a means of recording a recent decisive stage in our development. I hope that no partisanship of any kind will be found in them. The problems we face go far beyond the actions of a party, but political organizations are indispensable as tools.

But it is also true that this kind of political experience is hardly adapted to today's requirements. When threats to democracy are evoked, the spectre of fascism or nazism is automatically brandished: for several months and on various sides, the parties have been issuing repeated warnings on this score. I do not say that no such danger exists, but I find it very difficult to feel any lacerating anguish. I have reason to believe that old-style nazism and fascism got necessary support from German or Italian big business; I would like to know where any nazism in Quebec would locate such resources. I am as suspicious of fascism as the next person, but that should not distract us from other dangers present undeniably in all Western democracies.

With the rise of the great economic powers and the technocracies, the traditional parties are no longer adequate to embody practical politics. What possible influence can the timid voice of one citizen have beside the suggestions of the powerful and anonymous decisions? The state, of course, with its enormous budget and spending power, has important control devices, yet the policies of the state's technicians are scarcely intelligible to the ordinary man. No doubt some very laudable efforts have been expended in this regard: Mr Trudeau's government, distinguished as it is by concern with efficient administration, is also trying to shed some light on the technical data on which its actions are based. There have never been so many white papers. 'It isn't a government any more,' someone remarked to me, 'it's a publishing house.' He was exaggerating, of course. In any case, at a time when a praiseworthy concern for the fullest possible information and expert advice is being shown, party habits have barely changed. The last leadership campaigns turned up the same general declarations, the same abstract or sentimental programs. The sickness of our democracies inheres in this dichotomy.

If we stick faithfully to the democratic ideal, we must believe first of all in the original function of politics, bringing to light the basic choices of societies. Ideology as well as administration can put coherent goals into the life of society. Amid the increase of power bases and the swarms of opinions, the citizen needs the parties to present him with the broad alternatives – not objectives so general as to exclude further debate: one cannot disagree with such slogans as 'a just society,' 'a new Quebec,' or 'a prosperous Quebec.' If we want our democracies to survive and develop, the political parties must introduce plans – that is, broad objectives suited to capabilities – into the electoral stakes. It has been suggested that political parties could practise political education. This does not require courses or schools, or that the candidates run around the villages with the *Canada Yearbook* or Burdeau's *Traité*. Let them meet over specific aims and estimates of means: the voters will thus have a chance from time to time for self-interrogation on the problems and options of their society.

Many citizens see the program of the Parti québécois, and the way it has been worked out, as an important first step in this direction. It is still a rather timid beginning. One notes at first glance that many proposals and themes have been appropriated from the tides of opinion that have been whipping us up now for some time. Is it simply a case of plagiarism? Why is there no concern for participation as well? A party program is not to be judged on complete originality: in that case what would be democratic about it? It should be evaluated, and I come back to this word, on the basis of the coherence it offers for the aspirations of a society. To wrap occult strategies in solemn declarations drawn up for the occasion is the eternal purpose of public authorities; to make all choices without regard for contradictions, or the logic of the means, is the spontaneous desire of the citizen distant from public affairs. The primary function of a political program should be to guard against this double temptation of democracies.

We saw a good example of this in the debate surrounding Bill 63. The government in power suggested a choice while at the same time unable to be precise about its conditions and deadlines. On the other hand, certain opponents who demanded unilingualism were little concerned with the complex realities and planning methods. In this context has not the Parti québécois program on linguistic policy made available to many people a set of analytical principles in the tangled underbrush of loyalties, interests, and passions?

An expression of the profound but still vague aspirations of a people, an authentic political program, must evidence the concern to articulate the goals thus suggested to it. On the other hand it should also react on opinion as an instrument of criticism. The program of the Parti québécois can play this double role. It deserves, then, more than a relaxed party adherence: it invokes the freedom of democracy's dialogue.

PART FOUR

Autumn 1970: impasse?

The crises and the crisis

We can and must arrange and classify the many crises that have hit us during the last ten years. A primary task is to try to understand this country on the basis of what it has been able to tell about itself, through such apparently different events as De Gaulle's visit, the Montreal police strike, the demonstrations against Bill 63, and many others; this task brings together the symbols of the hopes and dilemmas in which Quebec has been attempting to fix its course over the past decade.

The immediate causes of these disorders have not been the same; they have not always involved the same elements of our society. Is it possible to find a common form in them? Can they be seen as symptoms of a deeper malaise, as in medicine a rash here, a pain there, an unexpected depression, or a sudden start, may eventually disclose a sickness that is gnawing at the entire organism?

The most recent crisis, that of the fall of 1970, forced us all to ask ourselves this overall question. Considering its most limited and easily discernible aspects, there was nothing in this crisis that was radically different from previous ones: how were two kidnappings, carried out by a few individuals, more serious than the Montreal police strike, and why did they this time justify the War Measures Act? One might think that this act was the last straw, or that something had to be decided and the time was right. After a variety of scenes and tableaux, social change and the Quiet Revolution had to come to an end. As in a theatre, the show had to close. The details of the last act might have been different – FLQ or no FLQ, War Measures Act or some other legislation gathering dust in the national archives, Mr Trudeau or Mr Bourassa – I have the feeling that none of this was basically very important. A society where rapid changes have occurred, but which has not absorbed these transformations at an equal rate, had to run up against a moment of truth whose pretext could have been anything at all.

If we take exception to this view of things it will be difficult to shed any light on the protagonists' attitudes and behaviour. This was not the first time the FLQ had weighed in, and its manifesto contained nothing that amounted to a revelation on Quebec's problems. Why then did it so

Excerpt published in the special issue of *Le Devoir*, 30 December 1970

abruptly arouse the sensitivities of so many of our fellow citizens? I see
no other explanation than that this was the sudden eruption, expressed
by a symbol that could have been quite different, of the bitterness and
hopes accumulated over the years, already revealed furtively in various
lights by so many other crises. On the governments' side, even before the
murder of Mr Laporte, there was the same general growth of awareness.
It is astonishing not to have more precise information about the enormous 'conspiracy' that was capable of causing the invocation of the
War Measures Act. Cabinet ministers who were busily adding up sticks
of dynamite and all kinds of weapons have since, at various times, done
quite a lot of subtracting. We know it now: the 'conspiracy' was nothing
but the convenient label to be stuck on an ambiguous social phenomenon
that could not be effectively controlled and reduced.

Diagnoses were presented on both sides. The FLQ supplied a plan for
finishing the drama of Quebec's erratic evolution over the past ten years.
To define its own role the government had only to turn it around. The
audience, Quebec society, joined the game of the end-of-year reports.
The FLQ manifesto evoked varied support, very warm or very hesitant.
Some people distinguished between *aims* and *means* as though we completely lacked any tools for political analysis except for this brief gospel.
It was a pretext, like the stone you throw into the water that generates
a series of circles that are less and less clearly defined but whose final
limits cannot be drawn. Conversely, with War Measures added to the kidnappings and the murder, other reactions appeared, just as vague but no
less tempestuous.

Men who had still been lucid the day before welcomed unconditional
authority. Parents denounced teachers. Unionists called in the police to
break up arguments. Priests formed a coalition against their bishop. Edi-
torial writers blamed defrocked priests. Winning fifty-two seats out of
fifty-two in the municipal election, the mayor of Montreal trampled in
his fury on those who had not been elected. If you showed the slightest
hesitation, even if only to show a personal appraisal of the tragedy, people replied that the time for philosophy was over, that it was the time
now for the police: and that it was too late to chat about 'the sex of
freedom.'

Thus, all the inhibitions of the last ten years of social change rose back
up to the surface. On radio 'hot-lines,' in conversations and speeches, the

educational changes that some people claimed had bewitched the young were debated again. The religious authorities were criticized for lacking firmness, for allowing the old-time religion to be changed too quickly. Foreigners, intellectuals, journalists were lumped together in accusation along with all those who had broken the peaceful silence of former times. Politicians felt the traditional basis of their power trembling and shouted their fear publicly, the better to confirm it. A large part of the population set out to repudiate the recent history of the collectivity and, at the price of police force, to wish the last ten years to be miraculously erased.

Perhaps we needed such a commotion to bring us to the realization that the rapid evolution Quebec has undergone since the last war, particularly since 1960, had not really been imagined. Not only was there a deep gap between the generations but, obsessed as we were with the spectacular revolt of the young, we had not taken note of the suppressed revolt of the adults and the old. Though most of us had been captivated by the commotions in our traditional life-styles, there were few who had accepted the profound structural alterations which must logically follow. Though social action had grown protean, our political personnel were still, with a few rare exceptions, those of the 1920s. Though the wide range of choices was a sign of our society's vitality, it did not offer sufficient guidelines for the Québécois not to be tempted one of these days to group themselves in opposing and hardened camps which, by their coherence in the abstract, bring about an arbitrary security. 'Keep quiet and let the leaders talk,' they would tell us at the worst moments of the crisis. The leaders were the FLQ on one side and the governments on the other. At last there were some clear and simple statements. Language no longer took the unbeaten path of hesitation, plans, nuances, and fragile hopes. History was taking a systematic and precise direction which, some thought, it should never have lost.

Must we be content with this rough accounting that was the October crisis? From now on will our society repeat, in other similar convulsions, the malady of change tormenting it? In any case, one thing seems obvious: the transformations in Quebec over the past fifteen or twenty years have not emerged with an overall significance.

Is evidence needed on this?

In a very brief period of time we have discerned the diversity of factions and interests that characterize all societies in the world. No doubt our collectivity has always had a variety of groups, 'states' and 'conditions' as they were called in the old days; but this plurality was fused from above, in authorities, customs, common values. What took centuries to happen and be articulated in other places has emerged here within a few decades. I see it beginning here with the last war, which brought us an artificial prosperity that had no roots in our economic infrastructure but caused a crucial alteration in our customs. Many of us had known and experienced the traditional styles of social integration: a great cohesion in local environments, even in sections of the cities where rural attitudes and customs had often been transplanted; elites whose authority had rarely been questioned, in principle at any rate. Social problems found their solution in small circles where political patronage came to top off forms of community assistance conceived on the same model. In thirty years these characteristics were reversed. Social problems have been defined on the national scale and become standardized to a certain extent. Patronage has had to come to terms with the technocratic rationale and bureaucratic anonymity. Antagonisms and factions came to light, sometimes in brutal fashion. Marginal groups, formerly enclosed in their own surroundings, lined up their solitude and anger. At the same time, the beliefs that were the foundation of traditional unanimity have been compromised. The decline of religious observance has won over the young and reached older groups as well. Less openly, day-to-day prospects on life's directions were blurred, without our being able to pick out, in any very clear way, new styles of existence.

I shall move on quickly now, as these things are already understood. The changes have been very rapid, and no doubt we must carry them out at this rhythm to make up for the age-old stagnation we were accused of in the 1950s. And in any case that is not the fundamental question. When a society transforms itself, especially if this happens in an accelerated way, it must somehow assimilate the disorderly evolution it is undergoing. Elsewhere, in older societies that are larger and more complex, there are braking mechanisms; occasionally, revolutions occur also, but the way is usually prepared for such change by the rise of a new class and a new power. Here there was nothing of the sort. We might have been able to compensate by the progressive emergence of an overall model of our collective development. But the men who had recently preached radical change for Quebec had left us with only very abstract goals: pluralism, opening up to the world. Since then, each crisis has tossed us back and forth between contradictory ideals. The workers in some industry or other, the teachers, policemen, or doctors, wanted to talk about salaries and incomes: they invoked parity with Ontario or the United States. They were given the explanation that Quebec was not a society like others. If they then oriented themselves towards the originality of Quebec, looking for a proper name to give it, such as 'independence' or 'unilingualism,' they were called to a wider understanding of the outside world. It was a vicious circle with no centre.

A model of development that belonged to us and could have let us evaluate the various changes failed to appear then, and we still lack it today. In the years to come, neither new waves of the FLQ nor new versions of War Measures will help. Nor will we create cohesion in Quebec by a return to the past or by a new religion. When a people reach a condition of diversity even in their day-to-day life, they must carry the consensus that brings them together to the level of politics.

Certain people, and I am one, became independentists for the very simple reason that they believe that our society could at least pull together the ideals and instruments capable of giving shape to the unusual changes still affecting it. But no doubt we are, for the moment, carried towards a more urgent and complex task. During the October crisis I found myself dreaming like everybody else, hoping for some kind of order in our situation, beyond the attempts of the FLQ or the police, one that would provide us with a plan for development. Not a voluminous technicians' report, but an inventory of our needs and of the transactions that were still possible among the scattered and diverse elements of Quebec society. New Estates-General? A government that would finally reach our people outside the rites of election-time? I really don't know. In any case, I would like to bear witness to the fact that change can be effected democratically, in such a way that we shall not be tempted once again to violate a declaration of human rights we have not even had time to proclaim.

Or must we go on waiting, as many people seem to think, until Quebec is actually dying, in the midst of a more dramatic crisis than that of October, in an immense display of fireworks from the left or the right? It is already very late.

Crisis and symbols

How can a collectivity shape its future?

I doubt whether anyone expects an outline plan for Quebec's economic development, or prophecies about our cultural future. I cannot do such things, lacking competence in such diverse matters. Anyhow if such projects are to appeal to the collectivity, they must originate in the collectivity as well.

Besides, the October crisis has taught us nothing new about the economic or other problems which continued, after it as before, to push us towards a more advanced planning for which we already had at our disposal wide technical knowledge and competent men of science. It is in a broader context that the crisis takes on meaning: it forces our examination of the primary conditions for the birth of a collective project, anchored on elementary co-ordinates we have no doubt known in the abstract, but which the recent commotion has finally made concrete for us.

In our societies it is rare for a single event to affect the entire population. A highway accident, a sports victory, a spectacular trial, a political declaration – these usually touch but a fraction of public opinion, or at most the event is broadcast unevenly through the various layers and sectors of our collectivity. Normally, interest and emotion are roused for only a brief moment, and the next day the news media suggest other occurrences that will in their turn hold our temporary attention.

But this time one event mobilized all of Quebec, almost from the very beginning. It was discussed everywhere, in town as well as in the country, by taxi-drivers as well as students. The radio gave the beat for this collective panting. A few individuals were able to hold the attention of an entire society in a state of tragic suspension for a period of weeks. One event became an extraordinary symbol.

Ordinarily, when we speak of 'social problems' we think in terms of the most material and visible aspects of collective life. Unemployment is defined in an economic context, the religious or educational malaise in terms of structures and organizations, the ethnic problem according to demographic co-ordinates or in terms of the inequality of powers. The political authorities themselves certainly feel obliged to formulate problems and sometimes to resolve them in terms of functional indices and planning. The less visible and less concrete aspects of the life of society are put aside, as a matter of course. In theory, dreaming is a good thing for the solitary individual, the poet or the artist, or for moments of leisure and privacy. We confuse the official and the rational. We forget that collectivities dream as well; that symbols, far from being some kind of residue of the economy or the organization, may be the props or even the goals of community life. We know how the advent of psychoanalysis disturbed views on man: it showed that beneath the play of reason explosive forces are outlined whose tensions are barely expressed at the level of articulated language and which are badly accounted for by surface intellectualizing and rationalization. It would be astonishing if this were not true, to some degree, for societies as well.

So many of the events that have occurred in Quebec in the past few years should have convinced the most rational observer of this. The election of April 1970 was different from the others above all because it introduced some particularly disturbing symbols into political debate. 'Vote Québécois,' as the partisans of independence put it, did not simply mean choosing an electoral program. The same went for some on the other side: those who sent for the Brinks trucks, for instance, were certainly not unaware of the powerful impact of symbols. Long before, at the time of the argument surrounding Bill 63, it was clear that this legal text was primarily a representation of the fear felt by many Québécois in the face of the danger of extinction. The bill did not aggravate the danger, but it symbolized it. The demonstrations that took place were more a celebration of the French language – at times funereal, at times joyous – than a political move, in the narrow sense in which we usually pretend we use this epithet. Going back even further, to the Quiet Revolution – why not? – André Laurendeau at that time was evoking 'a kind of self-confidence, the rise of feelings we have scarcely known in our history ... There are many of us,' he said, 'who believe that creation has become possible.' Creation? The word was explosive, because it called up something quite different from the political games whose interminable chronicle was pieced together by Robert Rumilly.

People will tell me that young civil servants, steeped in rationality, have undertaken the construction of a modern state. I am well aware of that. But we must remember, as they do, I think, the faith that inspired them. Besides, they have, in such a short time, done important things cold reason alone would have been unable to perpetuate.

Dreams long suppressed have paraded in the sun. In more sober societies an upheaval of this kind in the educational system or the liturgy
would have been impossible in so short a time. This can easily be verified by a look at the recent history of France or the United States. We
were basically freer than we thought: we were without a bourgeoisie
heir to long tradition, lacking a state burdened with old bureaucracies,
lacking profound attachments to conventions that for a long time had no
longer applied to us. We were savages.

Dreams were circulating freely. In the fall of 1970 they disappeared
into a blind alley.

Symbols. Particularly symbols? I will be accused of leaving the terrain
of facts and concrete data too quickly.

Among leftists I will be reproached for not first taking note of the
forces, classes, social movements, and economic imperatives that should
converge towards a supposedly 'revolutionary' explosion. They will even
tell me (it has happened already) that I am a 'Hegelian of the left.' May
I remind readers who are not familiar with Marxist holy scripture that in
the past the 'Hegelians of the left' were Marx's adversaries? You will find
more information about it in any paperback, so I will not labour the
point. Certain people need heretics; to help them identify with Marx,
someone has to don the garb of the enemies Marx selected for himself.
Well, why not? We can always read Marx during the intermission and
note, as we listen to the leftists' dialogues, that symbols are really very
important there.

But I shall not get away so easily. Messrs Trudeau, Marchand, Bourassa, and Choquette and other perfectly reasonable personalities will not
let me escape into the heaven of collectivities either. They have told us so
much about functional politics, economic growth, the vanity of flags and
nationalisms, that they must certainly have some kind of down-to-earth
explanation for us.

They have tried; that will be conceded.

Thousands of members of the FLQ, a training camp north of Montreal,
tons of dynamite, and stacks of rifles stored in every corner – some began
to wonder how people legitimately elected, as they say and as we say
too, could have waited for the kidnapping of Mr Cross and Mr Laporte
to give us this whole accounting of the dangers threatening us. We had
entrusted the safety of the state to their hands. Was it not dangerously
irresponsible of them to wait so long before putting together the various

indications of an 'apprehended insurrection'? Happily, the plot disappeared as soon as the police took an interest in it. Mr Laporte's kidnappers had bought their rifles that same morning in a shop where I imagine they sell standard kidnapper's equipment to whoever wants it. Why did they not take advantage of the considerable stocks ready for the insurrection? Were they anxious to economize as well? And then we were told that the FRAP was a front for the FLQ. On the day following this assertion we had to acquiesce in a linguistic debate. Doubtless the insurrection file was not absolutely complete.

By raising taxes a little, we will be able to recycle the technicians who prepared the file. A government that never stops reminding us that the time for dreams and ideologies is past, that it is now time for rationality, a government whose leader is a man as eminently reasonable as Mr Trudeau, will not fail to bring the closest calculation to bear on any future insurrection, real or apprehended. This first error in bookkeeping should not be pursued too rigorously. Like all of us, the governments had only symbols to serve as guides. So they shouted 'Fire!', but without looking very closely.

The danger of fire was much mentioned. One man, a priest moreover and a man I admire greatly, wrote in *Action* on 28 October 1970: 'When people fear their house is on fire it is a bad time to tell them that firemen are irritable, that they must examine themselves about the nature of the fire itself and about the mess firemen make.' That is very sensible, except that the question some of us asked timidly in public about a negotiation that might have saved Mr Laporte's life coincides with one that occurs to any reasonable fireman at the outset: is it a widespread fire or a false alarm? Whatever the case it is decided whether or not to bring out all the equipment, taking into account the risk of a massive mobilization of all one's resources without provision for the next time. One hesitates to galvanize the fear of all the surrounding neighbourhoods in case, because 'Fire!' is shouted thoughtlessly, no one can be found to believe in it and put it out. People of my age will remember reading in their children's books the story of the boy who cried 'Wolf!'

Messrs Trudeau and Bourassa stated they received tons of letters of approval. I believe them. If I went to tell my neighbour on the left that three armed men had been prowling around his house for days, I could easily persuade him to be very hospitable to the police and even, no doubt, have my neighbour on the right arrested. If I pressed him a little he would even write me a letter about it. Still, for future safety, it would be necessary for me not to have exaggerated in telling him about the threatening men on the prowl in his garden. 'Tomorrow, the victim could be the manager of a *Caisse populaire*, a farmer, a child.' So said Mr Trudeau. Symbols again, or at least figures of speech.

Let us return to symbols then, with fewer scruples.

Without giving a long lesson in sociology or philosophy, we may recall that, in the tradition of scientific social analysis, two tendencies have emerged progressively.

According to a first point of view, we explain collectivities from the bottom up: men have interests that come to them from 'production reports' of their society; they belong to classes, they are parts of organizations. In a word, they work. And when they dream, their ideologies take off from a ground made harder by their labours and conflicts. Who would disagree, even if he has not read Marx? As long as he has worked.

But there is another view of things, one that takes off from the reveries through which men – plumbers or doctors – bring down into their existence the most empirical ideals that are within them. To follow this analysis, it is not necessary to believe in a mysterious collective Spirit that hovers over societies. It is enough to recognize that men dream when they work and vice versa; to recognize too that if work has its consistency, its technology and organization, dreams pile up as well, and impose on groups of men a logic that, though less clear maybe than the other, still demands deciphering.

We must be very careful not to claim that one or other of the two readings is the more important. Leave that to scientific or political liturgies. Besides, the last elections in Quebec have illustrated this, without the need to cite any authors or collegiate orthodoxies: 'independence' – a symbol, a dream; '100,000 jobs' – a symbol and a dream as well.[1] Turn the two slogans around: you will find two sides of the same cloth, the one that makes up all the societies in the world.

Perhaps we can go further just once more and here only, without succumbing to the lengthy argument required in academic theses. Let us

1 Robert Bourassa himself confirmed this to reporters during a CBC broadcast ('Format 60,' 6 January 1971). Speaking about the creation of 100,000 jobs at election-time in April, he said he did not really intend to make an 'electoral promise,' but to 'dramatize' the problem of economic development in Quebec. What some voters had taken to be rational politics turned out to be dramatics.

present a kind of hypothesis that will be useful later on: between work and symbols, between rationality and dreams, speech is the way to articulate history and gain mastery over it. If it feeds on the desires and dreams that circulate among men, it can also tame them, subdue them in dialogue and schemes which in turn make possible the political community's existence. Assuring freedom and responsibility of speech to all, democracy implies that collectivities are not to be delivered up to unintelligible daydreams, just as it refuses to leave the problem of keeping them in check to force alone. Commonplaces, no doubt, but commonplaces are fragile things, like the reason that sleeps in them and whence at times it takes flight.

In this time of panic we have given much thought to the use made of speech in our society. Journalists, Radio Canada, intellectuals, 'theoreticians of democracy,' all have been abundantly criticized. Whatever aberrations may have been uttered, they give in their way a fundamental explanation. Not, of course, in the sense that too many words have been focused on the problems of our society. For then it would be necessary to give the bishops a prominent place among the accused, beside the committees of citizens and sociologists, journalists and union leaders. One would have to be a fool, or want to monopolize the floor for oneself alone, not to recognize that until now, in human history, men have been able to master their situation only by first giving it meaning through words.

We have talked a lot since 1960. But how have we talked? If the stupor that struck us in October was accountable by collective symbols, the tragedy was above all a cultural drama. We should not be afraid of this word, because it designates the mental equipment of a society, what it uses to analyse its reality, its dreams, and its plans. It was our culture that failed us at the hour of tragedy. Obscure conflicts, accumulations of fear and hatred, factional simplifications and idle talk caused the breaking out of scuffles that hindered articulate speech.

The explanation must be found, then, somewhere in the evolution of our culture, of our collective speech, over the last ten or fifteen years, those years that it suits us to call – symbols and words again – the Quiet Revolution.

Democracy and speech

Among the many often obscure pretexts furnished us by governments to sanction the imposition of the War Measures Act, one deserves our attention. At the beginning the federal Minister of Justice spoke of 'a kind of disintegration of the will of the people.' He returned to this later, insinuating that the hypothesis antedates the arrival on the scene of the few individuals who proposed to save Mr Laporte's life, that it had been accepted for a fairly long time, and remained the most plausible hypothesis once the 'parallel governments' and pseudo-data on the 'insurrection' had gone up in smoke.

An erosion of opinion. I accept this diagnosis completely. An indefinable malaise, much-entangled sympathies, a defect in the daily indifference of many citizens to the appointed authorities. This was not the first time, of course. Perhaps Mr Turner has read the long account published by Mr Trudeau at the beginning of a collective study on the 1949 Asbestos strike. After a long evocation of Quebec's history for the past hundred years, Mr Trudeau concluded: 'Certainly there were other major strikes in French Canada before the Asbestos strike, and there will be others. But this one was significant because it occurred when we were experiencing the end of a world, just at the moment when our social frameworks – worm-eaten because made for another era – were ready to burst apart. The date was crucial, not so much the place or the particular industry: chance could have had the strike break out elsewhere than at Asbestos. For at the time the Quebec proletariat had been brought by the logic of its own development to carve a place for itself in the community proportionate to its size and social usefulness.'[1] A similar diagnosis could be made for the crisis we have just lived through. This time it was not a worker group that challenged our society but a group of terrorists, and that, needless to say, made all the difference in the world. The social upheaval that was the result for democracy could no doubt have had a different cause; as in the Asbestos strike, 'the date was crucial.' Too many things had built up in the history of Quebec democracy for the crisis not to have manifested itself, in some way, for all to see.

1 *La Grève de l'amiante* (Éditions Cité Libre 1956), 90

To speak of 'an erosion of opinion' as Mr Turner did is, then, an exact diagnosis. Of course, I give the minister the benefit of the doubt. I assume he did not mean that because a certain social conformity had been compromised it was necessary to re-establish it by force, but rather that the edifice of democracy itself was cracking dangerously. We must therefore find out what opinion we are talking about here.

If I understand him correctly, the issue was a certain basic unanimity, a fundamental consensus which did not, at least on the surface, exclude opposition and conflict. No society can exist without differences, simply because of the existence of divergent interests, unequal powers, and a multiplicity of points of view. But democracy could not continue to exist without an underlying solidarity that in fact permits confrontation to appear and prevents any group whatever from feeling excluded from the area and rules of the dispute. The legitimacy of the state, then, is based on this consensus. The vote is not the way to achieve it, but simply the way to symbolize it in selecting those to take care of the political machine. In voting, citizens are invited periodically to bring into action the rules of the game, which they ratify by using them to promote their own divergent views on the orientation of the society in which they participate. Sending the question of democratic consensus to the ballot box means reducing to caricature a problem that is far more complex.

The most genuine tradition of democracy has never done this. If it has always jealously protected freedom of speech, for example, it is not merely so that the citizen can chat without fear about the Montreal Expos or Chinese ceramics. It holds that, by making society's problems and goals an endless public debate, men could find the very reason for the group adherence. Rather than impose unanimity from outside, as totalitarian regimes do, the democratic tradition has meant its citizens to make the experiment from within, testing it amid the freedom of their differences. In a democracy there is a life of opinion, an unending production of consensus. And when we say that opinion is crumbling we must not confuse its vitality with the loss of a dull, hypocritical uniformity of thought and action.

The democratic consensus is a fragile thing: it is so by its essence. It is enough to have a little acquaintance with history to know that it is never set once and for all within fixed limits and regulations, so that the police or the army would be adequate to restore it when social change threatened established convention. Nor, moreover, could we be content to allow the interplay of conflict and challenge without worrying about the climate that makes them possible: the free citizen of democracy is he who defends his own position as far as the problems of the world are concerned, while at the same time watching over the endless renewal of the consensus that allows such positions to be expressed. For where there is life and movement in opinion, and not rigid convention, the first reflex of democracy is to accept this vitality as a supreme value, as the very foundation of its legitimacy. Its reflex is also to work for its coherence: to so arrange it that no groups place themselves on the fringes, quitting the basic consensus, and, accordingly, constantly to expand the perimeter of legitimate speech. For example, if a new option appears (independentism, say), if previously voiceless groups adopt a previously unused means of expression (citizens' committees, say), it is the highest responsibility of genuine democrats to ensure that they find a place in the public orchestra of voices.

This is particularly the responsibility of the head of state. Like anyone else, he must defend firm positions. However, control of the power he exercises gives him the special duty of ensuring that everyone can find an echo in public opinion and thus take his part in the consolidation of consensus. Politicians often seem to forget this essential task. There has been much insistence of late from some of them here on rational administration, and I do not hold it against them: yet one would have liked them to show a little more concern, at a time of rapid evolution in structures and mental habits, for keeping open the circle of democratic speech. For if we want to contrast democracy and violence, as has so often been done during the course of the crisis, we must remember that violence consists of wanting to get out of the circle, or to close it at any price. In this sense, also, there is confrontation of two kinds of violence which, though antagonistic, are no less a threat to what is unique in the working of democracy.

From this point of view the factors of the crisis go back to long before the autumn of 1970. They should probably have been foreseen in the sixties. We were happy enough then to cry out the benefits of pluralism to the four winds. It seemed quite clear to us that individuals and groups should be able to announce their religious, artistic, social, and political ideas. We had become tolerant – or so we liked to tell ourselves. And we have been tolerant in a number of areas. In religion, for example, it seems to me that with a few exceptions believers and unbelievers have shown a marked ability for dialogue. The attitude of the Church leaders was very important here: their open-mindedness and discretion have helped avoid tensions and hardenings of position that many other societies have known in similar circumstances. However, there too there could have been much material from which to deduce monstrous 'conspiracies.'

It is chiefly on political grounds that pluralism has found itself compromised.

Consider the rise of the independentist movement over the past ten years. Everything was done to deny it a place in what I call the circle of legitimate speech. 'A tiny group,' people called it, denying it from the outset any claim to be representative. All the comparisons with nazism were trotted out, and in all possible circumstances. Incidentally, it must be admitted that we were in no position to call for democratic behaviour from people to whom all identification with democracy had first been refused. From another point of view, the attitude of Mr Trudeau's party, and particularly that of its leader, was damaging. Mr Trudeau has been talking about democracy for a long time and we must believe that his first loyalty is there. His is a very precise, formal brand of democracy and seems, moreover, to concern itself with the private life of the citizen. Respect for personal life and the discretion of the state are undeniably virtues of a democracy; but this respect and discretion are worth something in political terms too, and in what usually goes on outside our respective private nests.

I do not mean, and I hope I have made this clear, that Mr Trudeau and his colleagues should have become independentists because this political idea was beginning to make its appearance in Quebec. They had the duty of defending their federalist ideology with vigour. But Mr Trudeau and his friends were invested with legitimate power in Ottawa and this gave them an additional responsibility, that of safeguarding the climate of challenge with equal energy. They are fond of saying that if the people disagree with their attitudes they have only to kick them out at the next election. The principle is undeniable but inadequate: we had already said so, along with Mr Trudeau, in the days when it was Duplessis who held legitimate power. Taken on its own, this principle could lead to the following: once elected, you can do whatever you want between elections. Why is it necessary, then, to maintain an opposition within the walls of parliament itself? Is it an empty protocol? One might think so when Mr Trudeau, during the debates in the House, belittles the questions asked of him by the elected members who make up Her Majesty's Opposition. I repeat, from the moment he is elected it is the duty of a head of state not only to defend the positions that have won him his majority vote, but also to preside over the dialogues and political confrontations stirring up his society and giving it its democratic vitality. This is well known at other levels, in any associations that guarantee the existence of democracy. You are elected president on the basis of a program; once there, you are responsible for making sure every voice can be heard. You go even further: you attempt through your decisions to introduce new dimensions which, without necessarily being carried out to the letter, can be responsive to the wishes of opposing factions. Unless you do so your democracy risks becoming a dictatorship and your presidency a destructive factor in the association you have dominated temporarily.

If there is an independentist movement in Quebec, and if the last election produced the evidence that it concerns a large part of the population, this must be because we do, in fact, have a constitutional problem here. Independentists are not the only ones or even the first ones to have said it and to have repeated it. The Liberals and the Union nationale often reminded us of it before 1960. Mr Trudeau acts as though there were no problem. Five years ago many of us had not yet reached the solution of independence: we would have devoted the greatest interest to a consideration of a program of constitutional reform. If we have come to separation, it is because Mr Trudeau and his friends have refused to consider that the questions being asked by most Québécois might possibly have some basis. We would have been kicked out of the universities long ago if we had thus identified the legitimate authority conferred on us by our duty as teachers with scorn towards those who challenged our theories.

In the not-too-distant future, historians will show that Mr Trudeau destroyed the Canadian Confederation because he did not see its faults and propose serious reforms in time. When we accuse Mr Trudeau of not listening to the voices demanding rapid constitutional change, he replies that young separatists insulted him, breaking up his speeches in Quebec.

The majority of Québécois have never prevented Mr Trudeau from saying what he had to say; like all citizens who have examined their position openly for the past ten years, they are entitled to something other than this scorn that ought not to be extended even to an imbecile.

I have dwelled on this point, not to plead the cause of independence again but to recall, in this context of ours and in a non-theoretical manner, what I think is the essential duty of those with the legitimate responsibility for watching over democracy in this country.

It is easy to go on. After the last Quebec elections the supporters of federalism attempted some subtle statistical analyses. It had been advanced that independentism was a bourgeois ideology, but it was in the so-called people's ridings that the few Parti québécois candidates were elected. But never mind that – according to one federal cabinet minister, all these people had voted not for independence but to protest against poverty, housing conditions, working conditions. These are all things that can only be taken into account, no doubt, if one is a federalist. But to go on: 24 per cent of the votes in Quebec were cast for an independentist party, and the unfair electoral distribution returned only a few members and an insignificant official opposition – yet Mr Marchand was not content with this victory for his own ideology. He had to subtract on the one hand and cut away on the other, so that the 24 per cent was finally no more than 6 or 7. I read what he had to say and wondered, as I considered all the nuances, if I had really voted for the Parti québécois the day before as I had thought. To take democracy to the ballot boxes is to cut it off from its deepest roots; but Mr Marchand went so far as to dig around in the ballot boxes to sort out the voters' motives to his own taste. How then can one condemn those who no longer believe in democracy? Public men have shown little openness towards questions raised by the electoral process itself.

I could produce other examples applying, this time, to the government of Quebec. I will limit myself to one – but a spectacular one. One thinks immediately of the Bill 63 affair. I have already said that in itself this piece of legislation did not have the importance that many people ascribed to it. It is true nonetheless that in terms of democratic symbols it was unfortunate that the bill began by guaranteeing the rights of the English language on a continent where, so far as one knows, it is not seriously threatened and in a province where, unlike all the others, the minority language has always been respected. At a time when a tiny little people, who speak a strange tongue, badly at that, were beginning to have more doubt than ever before of the usefulness of their idiom, legislation was passed on the dangers of the disappearance of English. The paradox was obvious. For a long time now those who teach the French language here or who allow their children to learn it have been wondering whether they were not yielding to some archaic practice, condemned by history, whether they were not perpetuating unduly the obstacles that would ultimately prevent the next generation from entering into the life and processes of American civilization. To stay within the frame of reference of my own profession, there were a number of us who, in those morning hours when one sits, pen in hand, before a blank sheet of paper, hesitated, having qualms about writing in a language that would have to be translated for our descendants to be able to understand a little of what we had to say.

What happened? At the so-called National Assembly writers, critics, social scientists, and others were reminded that they had not been elected by the people. Of course not. Until further notice, literature and science are practised elsewhere than in the Legislative Assembly. From that time the types of buffoonery permitted to those elected by the people began to appear. The few – Messrs Lévesque, Michaud, Proulx – who tried to make outside voices heard received the worst insults in reply. Others went further and, in anticipation, made blood run in the streets. Please understand me: it is not the issue of the law's opportunity or futility that preoccupies me here, but the symbols involved, the way discussions and examinations were conducted, the scant attention given to objections from outside. Except in the case of a few members, mockery and invective took the place of attentive hearing and serious discussion. It seemed that legitimate power was just another faction. The score was tied, apparently; demonstrations were broken up, Bill 63 passed. Each demonstrator came home wondering what can be done when one lacks the time or aptitude to pursue a career as a member of parliament and has some concern for democracy.

I have not described everything that prevents a democratic dialogue in a society where, as Mr Trudeau has oft-times recalled, history has hardly accustomed us to this kind of exercise of power and responsibility. I may be criticized for not drawing examples from all sides, instead of only from those in power. I am not unaware that the most vain and hollow words, the most senseless dreams, have been at large throughout Quebec for the last ten years, and in other societies as well. But if we believe in democracy, we do not begin by putting the words of citizens or social groups and those of political authorities on the same footing. Otherwise we would have to admit that the National Assembly or the federal parliament have no more importance than a mob of protesters or a cell of conspirators. As soon as we claim to believe in democracy, we must insist that the words of political authorities be not only those of decision but also those of mediation among the various utterances expressing the intentions, interests, and conflicts of the collectivity. Thus I have presented examples familiar to everyone because they take on an exceptional importance as symbols of what could be called the official part of collective speech. A democracy begins to be sick long before the unintelligible noise of bombs is heard in opposition to the quite equally unintelligible words of the member for Iles-de-la-Madeleine, when official speech no longer echoes the mysterious language and symbols of a society, when it no longer knows how to calm and guide them into dialogues and projects in which citizens may recognize one another.

What is politics?

The collective planning of a future can never be identified primarily with a political party program. Not that political parties are to be scorned: they represent collections of opinions, interests, and ideas that have surfaced in a combination of historical circumstances and, at the risk of hardening, have sometimes gone under later on. But political parties have their own logic, originating in the needs of their struggle to reach power. They skim the projects emerging in their vicinity, even though they make more discreet accommodations with those more subtle forces at work in the collectivities.

When we examine the fate of societies we must also make a more intensive investigation of collective planning. The parties themselves invite us to do so. To do so quickly and remain within the context of Quebec's crisis, let us consider only a few examples close to home.

During the 1960s, when indigestible myths about survival were fairly sticking in our throats, certain politicians finally distinguished the elementary rules governing that administrative activity Saint-Simon was already talking about at the beginning of the nineteenth century. This was an important discovery, and the Liberal party of the period must be given full credit for having made it. Our people then accepted, even though it was in the rather confused decisions which drift into ballot boxes, that fate can be measured in terms of decisions and rational plans. Subsequently, we got more used to thinking this way, although perhaps it did not penetrate to the depths of everyone's awareness. When the issue was to make up for a delay in the education of our children that placed us last among all the Canadian provinces, or to tap our natural resources more exhaustively, objections were few. In principle, the policy bothered no one, particularly because at the same time we were being offered a well-defined individual freedom: even if the announcements came from Ottawa, these promises were no less well received. A society, without concern for custom and beyond conflicts, where atoms raised to the status of personality would cement a variety of associations under an impulse that might be called freedom – this, it was believed, was an absolutely democratic ideal.

These attitudes were appropriate as we emerged from a long lethargy in which custom had replaced the judgment and policies of reason and where, under the pretext of a community, the individual had been persecuted. In return we were tempted to attach less importance to the quality of those ties that, even following the destruction of traditional societies, form the indispensable common breeding ground of political projects. In Quebec, we had lived too much *en famille*: yet this kind of solidarity, though obviously in other forms, is still at the base of every political group. A man who is not from this region, an eminent theoretician of the liberal democracies, made some elementary comments under that heading which should be remembered: 'It is normal for us to carry over into our adult lives some things that are left over from that expectation of love, care, and help that was encouraged in our childhood ... This expectation is completely neglected in those social representations that take their cue from a bachelors' club: there, human relations are made up entirely of haggling, contracts approved and carried out, the justice of fair exchange. We seem to forget that the human species could not have lasted without the gift and that the gift is more essential than exchange.'[1]

It seems to me that the apparently paradoxical emergence of a Quebec 'neo-nationalism' in the last six or seven years must be judged with reference to that principle. It would be superficial to see it as simply a resurgence of the old nationalism: most of those who believe in it feel no nostalgia for the ways of thinking and living practised by the large family of those days; many have come to nationalism through the practice of trades and research in which rational criteria are crucial. One can only point out the need to recover that social community without which there is no political field. It is a difficult search, and a complex one, not without its exaggerations and dangers.

So two extreme temptations have threatened us and still lie in wait for us in our political 'productions' and in our ways of imagining a collective plan for Quebec. On the one hand we tend to insist too exclusively on rationality in means and ends, and this goes with a virtually exclusive devotion to the rights of individuals: on the other hand, the form of a mythical Quebec moves us to leave aside the conflicts of the interests and groups that belong to our society. These two ways of eluding the specificity of the politician typify the ambiguous condition of a collectivity like our own.

These days we talk a lot, and in every way, about democracy in Quebec. Perhaps we should recall an observation that goes back to the source of the political thought that has inspired the democratic tradition – that is, that politics is first of all the recognition of conflicts. This observation is so fundamental to the heritage of Western democracy that we find it written into our parliamentary institutions, where opposing parties are supposed to represent officially the conflicting interests and ideologies that haunt society itself.

Politics is born in violence, of struggles between economic forces, between privilege and enslavement. Far from emerging among individuals equal in right and awareness, political action emerges from among powers and struggles, and attempts to introduce a new kind of power and struggle.

1 Bertrand de Jouvenel, *De la politique pure* (1963), 78-9

Freedom is a curious thing. Men discover it only by stages. To be free is first of all to live the experience of a foreigner, to recognize oneself as different, even as the enemy of others. At the outset, freedom reveals itself in the form of selfishness. To affirm one's strength, the violence of one's grip on the world, is not only the typical experience of adolescence but one that is repeated every day, at every age and in all milieux. *Homo homini lupus est* – Hobbes was already saying it in the century when democracy was born. Democracy is not hypocritical; it repeats the saying and declares it still. In contrast, a totalitarian regime, whatever cloth it is cut from, always tries to mask the conflicts or to subdue them once and for all in an 'order.' This order is never other than that of injustice, because it implies that the social actors can be fixed in place, in the domination or subjection they have acquired through past struggle and violence.

In agreeing to step into the midst of these contests, democracy claims that it should establish there law – not a timeless law for abstract beings, who always turn out to be privileged classes and individuals, but a precarious law to be restored and held out unceasingly to new persons and communities. Law is defined and propagated in the midst of violence.

There is, then, a humility proper to democracy that goes back to man's most elementary feelings about love and hate. Psychoanalysts raise it readily. Here is an excerpt from something I read by chance: 'Establishing new human relationships always implies, in one who wishes to grow, the existence of a force sufficiently powerful to make the opponent take into account what that force represents. This is a commonplace, no doubt, but one that explains the failure of what we call reason in so many peace negotiations. This relationship of the right to be born with the confrontation of violence makes the purest causes impure, for violence is not deployed without destruction to the person who exerts it as well as to the person who is its object. Reacting against wicked desires relating to others, and developing in their stead feelings of friendship; in short, rejecting all hatred in the combat and struggle of politics is the task facing man when he is in contact with violence. There is no task more difficult, for the justice of the cause, and the horror we experience in recognizing our own wickedness, join together here to render difficult the salutary recognition of a truth that would deliver us – that we are not as good as we thought we were.'[2]

---

2 Louis Bernaert, SJ, 'Le chrétien et la violence,' *Christus*, 13, 52, act. 1966, 493-4, 49

To defend 'law and order' as though they were entrenched realities is thus a barbarous aim. We saw this during the crisis. Under the influence of fear, the most deprived citizen as well as the most secure wanted protection for the large or small circle where his selfishness and freedom found their roots. Once on the radio I heard a lady from the east end of Montreal, certainly not very well off, demanding the restoration of the death penalty: when her husband left for work in the morning, his lunch-pail under his arm, was he not in danger of becoming the victim of a terrorist? Fine, I said to myself, let's restore the death penalty. But when he comes home at night the husband will go on cursing the bosses and the capitalists and the politicians. That is the usual thing, and there is no need for the police to teach it to us. What are we going to do with this anger and the anger of so many others? Gibbets and more prisons? Or are we going to cover up with our hypocrisies, when faced with more spectacular forms of violence, the more secret hatreds and conflicts among which even the most deprived person comes at last to his accounting, his alibi, and his vengeance?

It is at this point, and the crisis has finally set it clearly before our eyes, that democracy is either secured or undone. Must we pretend to forget conflicts for the benefit of security? This logic leads us directly to totalitarian regimes endured equally by poor and rich. Conversely, must we welcome conflicts and use them to nourish a plan that tries as hard to include them as it does to surpass them? Then is opened once more the road of a democracy that recognizes that law is born of struggle, that peace is the utopia which justice tries to engender.

The FLQ did not recognize these choices either, judging by appearances. But, people will ask me, was it not violence incarnate? Bombs, two kidnappings, an assassination, what more do you need? I will reply that that violence attempts to be a magical reconciliation of all violence. Though democracy shows up conflicts, it allows them expression and leaves to men the business of internalizing and employing in their own fashion the law that surmounts hatreds. It entrusts to each the responsibility for naming justice in his own words. For conflict issues from economic systems but also from men; in this matter, no one is innocent just because he has no office on St James Street.

You are taking us back to human nature then, I will be told. In a sense, a primary sense, this is so. Freedom does not descend from the sky. It comes from us and it must come from all of us. The sermons of the preachers in retreats who used to talk to us of death and sin, standing with all lights out before a comic-opera catafalque, taught us nothing of liberty. The missionaries of more recent times without cassocks or surplices, who placed bombs and committed murder to wake up the people, follow similar methods. But peoples awaken slowly from their sleep; their conflicts and dreams take a long time to come together. It requires a terrible patience for the bitterness of all to be expressed. One should ask the desperate brothers, even if it seems naive, to contain the despair that haunts them, and is in us as well, faced with the election sport that is the surface foam of democracy; to think ahead still further to what has not been said about injustice and what we must help get said without end in the name of those who have not yet spoken.

To settle in a specific law, once and for all, the compromises of past violence; to join again, from a situation that is not everyone's, the many violences into one: this is also a denial of politics. The latter is not a coin or counter that one can keep in one's hand to use as an alibi or an apocalypse. The rule of political life and system for community life, democracy wants conflicts expressed to bring about the mutual recognition of men, and the changing of antagonisms into freedoms, yet always provisionally in anticipation of other freedoms.

Force or freedom: democracy places one within the other. To turn that into a dilemma whose terms would be strictly determined once and for all would be to bring history to a standstill. It would be leaving it to naked force, wherever it may come from, to put a stop to the future.

Conflicts and futures

Despair is not a political motive. It requires that symbols, words, and acts fall into place in accordance with sudden confrontations. A society is threatened with death pangs when it is divided thus into armed camps, not only because political projections are replaced by physical or verbal violence, but because aspirations, words, conflicts are no longer understood, mobilized as they are in schemes that remove their significance and authenticity.

If we want to return to democracy, or rather attain it, men who are still reasonable must, to the last detail, forbid persecution in the name of despair or reasons of state. It is particularly necessary to give the various groups in our society their legitimate voice and to spare no effort until political speech and the structures supporting it welcome these discordant aspirations. Discord is an atmosphere in which democracies with some spirit of adventure may find a process that is not straight as those of totalitarian regimes but is the more sinuous one of liberty.

Obviously this is not enough. A certain democratic tradition that has grown very abstract yields timid admission of the existence of conflicts, and freely defends the right of all to speak. It is less hesitant to name the antagonisms involved, particularly if they are groups in confrontation, and to discern the powers and aspirations seeking expression in the chequered vocabulary of our societies. We must try to go further, to locate at least in a rough way among the innumerable conflicts those that seem to characterize our collectivity in its depths. What fairly universal criterion can we use in doing this?

According to a desire now in fashion, all the world's societies claim to be pursuing their development. We are beginning everywhere to realize that this development must not be confused with economic growth, although this is not completely foreign to it. Raising the individual and collective standard of life and increasing productivity and jobs are activities not to be scorned. Yet they should in principle be subordinate to another kind of progress which concerns our way of life: the quality of the physical and social environment, human relationships, collective ideals. All societies are seeking a model for their development in which generally debated values can pull together the imperatives of economic growth and the demands of moral progress, a model that can settle essential conflicts, in the field of revenue as well as in that of ideologies.

Quebec has experienced a variety of concepts of development. One last time, let us agree to be reminded of history.

The first and most durable representation of the development that we have undergone put it all in symbols. As Quebec was deprived of indigenous economic power shortly after 1760, there remained magic and images. And it made great use of them. Lacking control over tougher decisions, we could maintain 'our language, our tradition, and our laws.' Contemplating Anglo-Saxon factories from afar, Msgr Paquet and others had carried us on to higher things, towards the victories of the spirit. Maintaining the symbolic universe had turned into a national industry, the only one that really belonged to us. Of course, these symbols quickly became clichés; the language carrying the message became superficial, thin, compromised. Poets, usually from the cities, exalted the virtues of the mythical peasants of their time, and the glory of departed conquerors; they were echoed by politicians in charge of a power with no significance beyond guaranteeing more real yet foreign powers – the paired words and values of two versions of official impotence. As in the poem where, after evoking the shadowy and painful memory of Mother France, Chapman consoles himself on the shoulder of the Lieutenant-Governor of the Province of Quebec:

> Still, we forget the splendid warriors
> Whose all-too-easy yoke our fathers knew,
> When, to replace those early governors,
> Our people doth engender men like you.[1]

These words, which were neither those of real powers nor those of real dreams, were infinitely far removed from the most intimate situations and resentments of the people. For collectivities as for individuals, symbols need to be ceaselessly animated by what is not themselves, by demands issuing from lower down. Failing this we have a juxtaposition of the abundant but pointless curses of our fathers and the paternal rhetoric of our poets and politicians who had 'done their classical course.' Deprived of those powers which challenge words that were too reassuring, and which give poetry and economics their just place, we were bemired in symbols that were not expressed and in words that claimed to express them.

In 1960 we committed ourselves in a second phase. Certain people became aware – and this emerged at the political level – that it was possible to come to terms with reason, power, and ideals. We quickly learned to talk about growth, investments, administration, and so on. Sons of illiterates or hucksters had learned all that in the United States, England, or France; they announced it to their students or whispered it to cabinet ministers. Public enterprises were created or those already existing were given fresh impetus. Engineers constructed dams on the Manicouagan in silence and poets articulated what they had done. A society was sending its sons to school to learn more technology and poetry. But what seemed to be a new departure in the direction of an original development model

1 'À l'honorable Augustin-Réal Angers,' *Les Feuilles d'érable* (Montreal 1890), 18

was cut short. We have created public companies of economic growth but have not entrusted them with too much money: just enough, probably, to keep poetry its place. We tried to regain some control over our natural resources but we soon stopped short along the way; we used to abandon them to exploiters who had been quite happy in the past to take them with the blessing of Duplessis, but now a federal cabinet minister gives our money to American businesses so that they too will kindly come and settle among us.

To all appearances at least, we finally clamped the circle of our dream life to the life of reason. But it is not that simple. Formerly, our speech, our poor way of voicing ourselves, took symbols and tamed them. It also prevented them from taking shape as a horizon and an ideal. It carefully avoided identifying the forces and conflicts in our society. Afterwards, and only recently, our speech has begun to challenge these symbols, but also to abandon them in the shadowy realms of ill feeling or poetry. A dangerous antagonism has gradually arisen. On the one hand, dreams have run loose in the streets. On the other, governmental policy, swollen with dreams in 1960, cast off its previous motives with the exception of bread-and-butter issues – both products, incidentally, which, like jobs, are getting scarce.

Dreams were also following the path of clandestine politics. Increasingly numerous marginal groups began to create new forms of power: citizens' committees, ACEF, fronts of all kinds. From the summit of legitimate power they were brusquely told they were asking for the impossible. Perhaps. But dreams join forces with reason only when spontaneity of participation makes its link with the political processes. Why did the governments not understand this and why did they not, at one stroke, speed up the reform of administrative and legislative institutions better adapted to patronage and bureaucracy than to participation?

The same could be said of some student unrest. The students were not the first to claim that our schools are often 'course shops,' and that universities are based on decrepit structures for which profound reforms are being demanded throughout the entire world. What official power has really taken up the challenge? Why should we be surprised if from then on demands became utopian and, as they say, unworkable? Or if they have drifted towards a passivity that augurs no better than the vociferations of our society's takeover by the next generation?

There has also been the rise of the Parti québécois. But it had to unite so many accumulated dreams, so many people representing all viewpoints. This party was, and still is, an assemblage of the most spontaneous of hopes, a social movement pursuing a wide diversity of goals. It would have been a sign of its leaders' greatness and courage if they had given a new form to Quebec politics. But the Parti québécois found itself suffering from an excess of functions. We must expect in a normal society to find a plurality of tendencies and levels at the heart of living, conflicting forces. Moreover, we understand that such a concentration of aspirations gave the April 1970 elections a meaning that passes beyond the usual electoral rituals. The disproportion between the Parti québécois vote and its official representation in the National Assembly, and the gap thus opened between dream and official speech, swamp the narrow concern of electoral reform: in this we must see a dazzling overall indication of the many deficiencies of our democracy. Another symbol was thus added to all the others that expressed the despair many of us felt.

In one of its rare moments of privilege, Quebec will thus have recapitulated in a very short space of time the dialectic that is inherent in the development of the West. The challenges and the fluctuating responses to them have been lived and summed up here in a microcosm. In the various analyses made of the case of Quebec, no one is too sure how to qualify us. Colonized? Underdeveloped? The most diverse adjectives are dragged in from all over the place without anyone ever succeeding in pinning down our uniqueness or our place in the universality of the planet's problems. Stuck in the northern half of the American continent, but foreign to America as well, let us admit that we are a testing ground. In this sense we are important to the entire Western world: for want of a better, this is our first opening to the universal. I do not say this for reassurance. I scarcely think the problems outside our borders relieve us of our responsibilities or that we discharge, with one blow, the responsibility for a confrontation between Ottawa, Washington, and Paris. But no society, no man for that matter, is the bearer of problems of his exclusive making.

In Western civilization dreams and reason have been in opposition for a very long time. Theoretically, power has always claimed a monopoly of reason. From Machiavelli to Louis XIV, from Robespierre to Guizot, from monarchies to revolutions, from restorations to republics, reason has increasingly been the supreme guarantee. Equally, in business, factories, and shops, the capitalist entrepreneur has wanted to represent the point of view that dominates all others because, in the calculations that bring together so many diverse factors in production, someone has to make the decisions. Decision is coherence: one can accept such a definition of reason without serious reservations; it is as good as many others. It is true nonetheless that we have had to put aside other kinds of reason: reasons that direct the calculations of the worker or the farmer, elector's reasons, reasons of the small elite groups kept on the fringes of power, trade union reasons, and many others. And dreams as well, for power feeds on images. According to the old political economy textbooks, the entrepreneur was motivated by 'the maximization of profit.' We confused the logic of the system with the aspirations of those who made the decisions; maximizing profit is a way of getting work out of a machine on which one's ambitions depend – specifically the pleasure, old as the world, of dominating others. There, for some, power meets the dream.

The reasons and dreams of others, then, have built up in withdrawal – an immense reservoir that neo-capitalism, opening the floodgates of massive production but also those of wages for certain categories of workers, has been able to use. Stimulated by advertising, the desire finally found expression. But it looks as if consumption has not succeeded in conveniently erasing all dreams and all desires. At the same time that it offered satisfaction, it created symbols to further excite our dreams and desires.

For the moment, in the United States, in Quebec, and elsewhere, we are all running on the same course. When students tell us, quoting Marcuse, that they are shocked to see workers rushing off to shopping centres to buy everything and nothing, they must obviously be reminded that for many levels of the population of Quebec or the United States, consumerism is a new thing and the young are old as consumers of food and culture. Nausea has not reached everybody yet. But, with or without Marcuse, it is becoming more widespread for many people. This is particularly true among the bourgeoisie, and it shows that revolutions are no longer exactly what Marx foresaw. Not that the bourgeoisie are making new revolutions, but their children, at least as long as they don't get too old, give a rather hazy representation of it. Satiated with well-being, they become hippies or something of the kind, hoping to find lower down the dreams that are not expressed higher up. Untamed by Western society, dreams finally form a marginal society – a margin that is ceaselessly expanding.

A special issue of *Life* estimated at several million the number of young Americans affected by the hippie life-style. But where does the phenomenon stop? The younger generation in its entirety, even in the farming or working milieu, finds itself implicated in some way. Parents and educators know this: so do drug-pushers and politicians. As a rule, we only want to see clear manifestations in such a life-style that allow us to define it as a marginal phenomenon. But the margin is such that, as in so many other things, it is becoming impossible to understand what roots are feeding such a growth.

There is a centre, nevertheless, a place where the phenomenon is more densely concentrated than in the fringes and can thus be better comprehended. On a visit to some hippie communes in California, Edgar Morin made the following observation: 'What happens in youth is the joining and the amplification of currents that were already crossing adult society, but each separately and which, because of this amplification and function, bring about a rupture. Thus the return to nature becomes "Let the sunshine in," the thirst for enjoyment becomes "Paradise now," the search for happiness becomes an aspiration for another life, individual need becomes anarchy, community need becomes communist, and the whole thing becomes revolutionary.'[2]

The young push further ahead, and more up to the surface, the desires and nostalgic feelings already expressed in other ways by the previous generation. The conventional haunts of the serious are being encircled slowly by the dream that has long been repressed. The authorities and the rationality which has served as security for them are in danger of being carried away little by little, despite the flattering rhetoric with which we gratify youth. If we don't watch out, the time for radical confrontation which could be the typical revolution of our times will not be far off, a revolution very different from those of France or Russia – a confrontation at the level of the symbolic magma where dreams are mingled with conflicts and power is stripped of its customary guarantees.

2 *Esprit* (November 1970), 526

But it is not the task of political analysis to expect or hope for miraculous catastrophes. Spectacular revolutions are always just a hasty catching up with what was not foreseen and achieved in the normal course of history. And then, if the dream is abruptly liberated in agnostic liturgies, new powers and new reasons are improvised too quickly as well. History must follow a different curve if we want it to be inhabited by free men.

What is to be done?

Crises, whether personal or collective, should not be given more than they can return. We have got a great deal already if we can find in them the motive to fall back on some elemental intuitions and an opening, one that is as large as possible, on the future. If it is true that the October crisis placed us more distinctly than ever before a drama that is blurring the symbolism of a society, we must use it to throw light on our near future, and in this same way.

As I have already said, I have no contempt for the reasoning applied to problems of economic growth. A plan would be very useful to us in this or any winter of unemployment and deprivation. What is the economic future for Quebec? What roles can the state, public and private enterprise, our co-operatives and unions play? These questions are dispersed across numerous studies and reports, and must be brought together. In the quarrel between professions of faith and professions of reason, a circle can be drawn of imperatives and possibilities, a circle where conflicts, dreams, and plans for the future can find the place for their opposition and reconciliation.

It would be too simple to suppose, however, that once the circle has been drawn we could then just splash about in the space left for dreaming. Economics is not a closed book of rationales and technologies. Growth, that which can be translated into indices and factors, requires subtler motivations. Symbols and feelings are involved in the process of raising productivity and standards of living.

How, then, can the connection be made?

Beyond myths of abundance, our Western societies are looking for new life-styles where work and responsibility would no longer be alien to consumption. Faced by complex and anonymous technical assemblies, man seeks refuge in a private life in a very tight circle. Or else, lacking the lessons that only daily responsibility for concrete problems can give, he dreams of transposing to society as a whole a miraculous spontaneity that cannot be found. The most typical revolutionary dreams of our time arise out of feelings produced by technological societies. There is a 'crisis of values,' as we hear repeated on all sides. But new values will not come to us one fine day as by magic, unless we rely on the periodic reappearances of totalitarian regimes, where new values take root amid the citizens' solitude and powerlessness by a promise of contact with collective values on condition that the citizenry accept a greater servitude. There is another way to make the new values emerge: it means leaving it to the citizens to sketch a definite form for it by degrees through more intensive participation in institutional management.

Participation: the word is worn out already, and after a period of great popularity when it seemed to be the universal panacea, it now runs the risk of being filed away with old recipes and down-at-heel political slogans.

If we do nothing to modify the structures and means of decision making, citizen participation in public bodies or the administration of businesses is nothing but a vain exercise which in the long run will fool no one. There is today an opposition between the necessary rationale of means and ends on the one hand and on the other episodic feelings mixed up with values. Numerous committees and councils are thus created to represent various groups and interests, but all this chatter does nothing to change the basic problem. We manage only to complicate the processes of formal democracy.

Participation is another thing altogether. It consists first of all in generalizing the idea of an experimental society. This is not a new idea, since it is found at the very core of our Western civilization. From science to economics, from theatre to psychology, our civilization has always imagined its progress in terms of schemes to be put to the test. For a long time now this practice has no longer been limited to the machine and, particularly in business, it bears on human relations themselves. Citizens must henceforth be invited to participate in this kind of experiment. Participation is generalized creativity or, if you prefer an expression that is more conventional but more ambiguous, a generalization of entrepreneurship.

From now on certain elements of collective life will lend themselves particularly to such attempts.

First of all there are the administrative structures of the state itself.

There is a tenacious myth throughout the West that should be denounced. We are forced to choose between the state, in principle bureaucratic and costly, and private enterprise, endowed, also in theory, with the faculty of innovation and the virtue of lower cost. Leftists themselves give in to these simplifications by demanding controls, rules, and committees as though socialism did not itself essentially value the spirit of enterprise. I know that the state is often less profitable than private enterprise, first of all because in our so-called liberal societies it has to pick up, one by one, remains of what was profitable for the entrepreneurs of yesterday. It sometimes labels as communal property whatever is no longer of interest to innovators and puts duties and taxes on it. But why does it not set off on new paths more frequently?

I also know that, in the structures of the state, bureaucracy is further advanced than elsewhere. According to the conventions of the old liberalism, watching over the common good presupposes the existence of detailed hierarchies and anonymity. But why can we not bring into the precincts of officialdom mechanisms that would be more favourable to a generalization of entrepreneurship? It would be enough to form travelling teams, teams that would be mobile like today's problems and society, who would be given the responsibility for carrying out specific projects. They could be judged later, after their efforts had been put together by imagination and technology. Arthur Tremblay, a senior civil servant whose rich experience is well known, has made some very interesting suggestions in this regard.[1]

1 In a remarkable statement to the congress of the Institute of Public Administration of Canada (9 September 1970) which should be widely publicized. I will restrict myself to reproducing the following extract: 'One might imagine that, above a certain level, a civil service career would provide a choice between, on the one hand, what I might call a "regular career," and, on the other, a career of entrepreneurship. In the Quebec system the regular career would correspond with the professional classes, assistant managers, or directors. Advancement in the regular career would continue to be made according to the present criteria. Access to the management would be by contractual decision whereby a civil servant would take on for a given period certain management or creative responsibilities laid down in a well-defined program and with mutually agreed conditions and benefits. In exchange for the

Obviously I do not mean that tomorrow morning we should remake all administrative machinery in this way. The idea of experimentation suggests methods of checking and evaluation. Choosing a few typical sectors, allowing them scope for action, and conducting observation there in the hope of being able to generalize afterwards without literally copying what has already been stated to be an effective way of working and joyful creation – that would be a concrete process, a historic one, from which routine as well as magic would be excluded. We could thus move away from those reforms that claim right away to be universal, radical, general, and that end up as computer charts to be stuck on the walls, or as edicts. Beneath their juridical and rational exterior (ratified, moreover, by committees), these abstract reforms meet those projects of absolute revolution where spontaneity would make for us, beyond the vain gropings of politics, a society without authorities, without conflicts, and without classes. (This remark is worth noting for the examples I shall be presenting later.)

In the academic world, to take another area of our collective life involving a large part of the population of Quebec, besides principles and structures there are the services of the Department of Education and the Quebec Teachers' Corporation. At a level that I know more intimately, that of the university, there has been no shortage of reports and committees either. It is agreed that all that was necessary. But as we have often said, it is up to us to create an academic milieu, something other than those abstract, over-administered boxes where our young people are confined for long periods of time to make up for the meagre educational resources that existed before 1960, or to spin out an original form of unemployment for as long as they possibly can. From the CEGEP to the university, if you want to create milieux where the young try out responsibilities while being initiated to the symbols and techniques of adult society, courses must be mixed with time spent at responsible work. Get students to create something as soon as possible, like the craftsmen of old times; make them do work that has some meaning

risk implicit in a formula of this kind, the higher-grade civil servants could insist not only that they be given additional remuneration for their management function, but also that they be allowed to exercise initiative and creativity and that the final judgment of their performance should not be laid down right at the outset by rigid supervision of their actions.'

other than producing marks to be stuck on to bits of paper and immediately stowed away in the college attic. This would surely be the most concrete way, and obviously the most complex as well, of minimizing the break between the educated leisure of the young and the poor labour of adults, of refusing to hallow an irreparable gap between the generations on the pretext of making up for Quebec's economic and academic delays. The young generation is bored in the midst of culture and the adult pays the price of the game without understanding a thing about it. But we will achieve this only on condition that we stop dreaming, alone or in committees, of new and sudden overall reforms that would end quickly in abstract structures or manifestos. Why not let several sectors of the teaching profession, at the college and university level, try to carry out pilot projects that would be concerned equally with pedagogy in the strict sense of the word and with life-style and a kind of social commitment? I would say the same, moreover, for scientific research, always on condition that the observations that were made were put before the public.

Now let us turn to a third illustration, one that is, apparently, as foreign to students as the latter are to those who administer the state. My illustration is taken from the agricultural world. It is well known that here in Quebec we are the victims of an old ideology that gave privileges to the habitants. For fifteen years we have been denouncing this old dream in at least as many books, articles, and talks as were required to create it. Just taking into account the amount of paper scribbled on, Msgr Laflèche and many others have at last been surpassed. But the rate of unemployment and the number of people on social assistance of all kinds remind us that we are barely further ahead. So some organizations are proposing the setting up of temporary experiments, beyond any general plan to be applied to all the world or even to Quebec, in which farmers would combine the cultivation of land and forest in accordance with carefully delimited projects they have worked out themselves. Such would be a kind of agricultural revolution not described anywhere in books, reports by ministers of agriculture, or the FLQ manifesto. Why not let them do it in a few villages and have the experiments openly evaluated for the benefit of the entire population?

One could, I repeat, cite many examples. At the time of the recent reforms in the field of health and welfare, it was suggested that more room should be left for community planning: why not permit several departures in this direction as soon as possible? Possibly community health services in an urban neighbourhood? Or an attempt at community administration by a group on social assistance in a village or one of the concessions outside it? I do not need to mention again the fruitfulness of the co-operative model: with the AECF and a variety of other enterprises, a new attitude has been taking shape over a number of years that values the variety of endeavours where structures too rigidly defined from above have been avoided and room has been left for what I call *creativity*.

My proposal is a very modest one – that experiments should be set up as soon as possible in certain sectors sufficiently populous to reveal the entire life of a society in all its major aspects: projects that are unambiguous and controversial enough to gain the attention of the media as well as that of civil servants and hippies, where the difficult union of dream and reason, symbol and work, would be put to the test. We would then be better able to discern the presence of dreams of compensation as well as motives and reasons that serve as alibis. We could also catch sight of what would be the structures and the style of a new society and those values that we speak of too often for an abstract future. For, as I hardly need emphasize, opening the road to creativity will not volatilize conflicts of power and classes. These conflicts will be better limited and better defined. Then a homemade socialism will find unambiguous strategies that can be debated by the entire population of Quebec.

I am sure you understand that the creativity of which I speak has nothing to do with recent admonitions to divert energy and dreams towards some forms of compensation. We must emphasize this because all words contain snares and delusions and because after having announced an insurrection for the fall, several cabinet ministers suggested creation for the spring: parcel out of the land around James Bay or northern Quebec, for example; or stimulate perhaps a broader creativity but at the level of culture or language; in other words, work around the problem so as not to disturb the old stalwarts. Thanks very much. It is from the bottom and the centre, not the top, that creation must confront dreams and powers. Only a nation is large enough to conceive and carry out our projects. We no longer want a vast kindergarten for marginal creation.

Despite all this, it would be perfectly ridiculous to propose a parallel line of action for American or French society. The intricacies of economic power, administrations, and agreements of the left or the right are so complex that one would easily agree to make these suggestions a program of social psychology, of group dynamics to sandwich in between the still loose links of edifices whose solidity comes from their very complexity. But in a society as simple, as backward as they tell us Quebec is, it would be enough that from the various horizons – from those I have indicated and many others as well – come experiments in which democracy confronts creation and rationality so that the effect of their propagation wins over the entire collectivity.

I have kept the last paradox till the end. Creativity is not enough for our ideal. When people talk to us about the need to 'create new values,' we must hesitate a moment. Are the values as new as they say? During the October crisis, which was prolonged less visibly into the winter, it would have been fallacious to believe that, thanks to the FLQ and the War Measures Act, we were at last able to distinguish between new and old values. In regard to questions about values especially, we must not give in to the logic of armed camps, no matter from what side we are pushed to do so.

The paradox of the fall is that of our Western societies at their present stage of evolution. We claim the right to creativity but also a certain stability in the life-styles, ideals, and relations experienced by men. This second side of intentions is as present in hippie communes as is the first: it was already inscribed in the apparently more innocuous dialectic of leisure and work proper to the middle classes and the bourgeoisie. Sociologists have revealed it as part of the American society next door.[2]

Quebec has shown its greatness in having confronted these antagonisms, slowly in its distant traditions and more dramatically during the recent crisis. The presence of the past, the desire for absolute innovations: there is the mark of our origins and our distinctive singularity. When you get down to basics, are there any really new values? Is what we call creativity anything other than the public manifestation, concrete realizations, of what has been contained for a long time in dreams? Does not speaking of values mean evoking aspirations that have been silently ripening, so that the organizations and plans that express them in the

2 See R.A. Nesbet, *The Quest for Community* (1953)

end do not depend on feelings of the moment which, because of that very fact, would have no future?

Are these vain metaphysical speculations? Can someone explain to me why young people, who are apparently so scatter-brained and so foreign to the older generations, speak of Quebec with an affection that few nationalists of the past would have dared proclaim, and why people who are the most detached from our traditional values are paradoxically the most concerned to find a future for them? Also why, to those who look for traditions, the October crisis found for opposition only a recreation that was more openly dedicated, in appearance, to the past? These are battles of tradition which end by suggesting the hypothesis that the new values could very well be traditional ones.

For my part, I believe that the values of the future are not *created*. They spring up like plants in the light, through a slow, obscure process of maturation in the silence of the earth. Quebec has something original to say about that. That is what I call independence: a conjunction, for us, of creativity and memory.

In the fall of 1970, a people, who are not under-developed in the sense that the word is used in theories and not developed either by those same criteria, put up terrorism and their oldest, deepest feelings in active opposition to one another. A little people they are, that could not be ranked, despite all the efforts of the past ten years, with clearly defined colonies or in the confusion of American prosperity, or even in the residue of the British Empire that is Canada. A people that has invented nothing that is the least bit official, like democracy, literature, capitalism, development. A people from nowhere, a people with no category or no status in diplomacy or in the system. On reflection, it is a privileged situation. While elsewhere people are filling their heads with rationality and dreams, with powers and symbols so complex that they can perhaps never be untangled, our slim pickings allow us to calculate and conceive only very simple future development.

One fine day, perhaps poor people like us will be able to invent an original form of democracy that springs from their very smallness. Who knows? For centuries we have spoken a doubtful language, not so as to end up as footnotes on the pages of Marxist or democratic textbooks, but in order to bring to the surface questions and answers that richer and more knowledgeable countries need in order to bring some shading into their lefts and rights. That would give meaning to a long survival, an impatient vigil. That would entitle us to an independence which would not be like that of others.

For peoples, as for individuals, obtaining access to the universal is first of all choosing for oneself the doorway that leads in.